Mystery at Shildii Rock

To Kim

When Scott is older I hope he enjoys "Shildii Rock" as a bedtime story. Having his mom read to him will be a fond memory he will keep for life.

All the best

Mystery at Shildii Rock

Robert Feagan

A SANDCASTLE BOOK
A MEMBER OF THE DUNDURN GROUP
TORONTO

Editor: Michael Carroll
Designer: Erin Mallory
Printer: Webcom

Library and Archives Canada Cataloguing in Publication

Feagan, Robert, 1959-
Mystery at Shildii Rock / Robert Feagan.

ISBN-13: 978-1-55002-668-9
ISBN-10: 1-55002-668-2

1. Gwich'in Indians--Juvenile fiction. I. Title.

PS8561.E18M97 2007 jC813'.54 C2006-904611-5

1 2 3 4 5 11 10 09 08 07

Conseil des Arts du Canada
Canada Council for the Arts

We acknowledge the support of the **Canada Council for the Arts** and the **Ontario Arts Council** for our publishing program. We also acknowledge the financial support of the **Government of Canada** through the **Book Publishing Industry Development Program** and **The Association for the Export of Canadian Books**, and the **Government of Ontario** through the **Ontario Book Publishers Tax Credit program** and the **Ontario Media Development Corporation**.

Care has been taken to trace the ownership of copyright material used in this book. The author and the publisher welcome any information enabling them to rectify any references or credits in subsequent editions.

J. Kirk Howard, President

Printed and bound in Canada

www.dundurn.com

Dundurn Press
3 Church Street, Suite 500
Toronto, Ontario, Canada
M5E 1M2

Gazelle Book Services Limited
White Cross Mills
High Town, Lancaster, England
LA1 4XS

Dundurn Press
2250 Military Road
Tonawanda, NY
U.S.A. 14150

To my children, Robin, Joshua, Michael, Tandia,
and the memory of Keith Allen Attattahak

Acknowledgements

Although this book is a work of fiction, Gwich'in legends, as well as the names of friends and respected elders from Fort McPherson, have been incorporated into the story to recognize the wonderful people of the Mackenzie Delta. Some events have also been based on incidents that took place while my family lived in Fort McPherson and Inuvik.

I would like to thank my parents, Hugh and Marj Feagan, for sharing their memories. I would also like to thank Rachael Villebrun and Bertha Francis for their contributions.

Chapter 1

Robin Harris was jolted awake as his chin bounced off his upper chest. Opening his bleary eyes wide in the initial moments of confusion, he tried to remember exactly where he was. The outline of his father's back at the front of the boat came into focus and the last cloudy remnants of sleep faded away.

He had been slumped in the bottom of the boat, and as he pushed himself up onto the wooden plank that served as a seat, he realized just how uncomfortable his position had been. His legs were stiff and his neck ached at the back where the muscles had been under strain as his head lolled forward in sleep. He noticed a large wet patch on the front of his sweatshirt and spied a shiny string of drool that still clung to his chin. With a quick, embarrassed glance at his father, he wiped the spit away with the back of his hand. A shiver passed through his body, and he wrapped his arms across his chest. He surveyed the passing shoreline to determine their exact location.

The day he had awakened to was much different than when he fell asleep. They had been upriver visiting some of the few remaining fishing camps of summer. The fall air had been cool, but the intensity of the sun had brought a cheerful balminess that had overtaken the coolness of the season.

The Peel River had been smooth and pristine, with sparkles and warmth given birth by the sun. It was with the heat on his face and bright reflections in his eyes that Robin had nodded off to sleep, soothed by the wind and rhythm created by the movement of the boat.

The sky was now grey and bleak, the air cold and wet, while the river had become dark and gloomy and had waves of considerable size. The chop was harsh, and the eighteen-foot Royal Canadian Mounted Police ply craft speedboat bucked with the concussion of each and every impact. Robin realized it had been the turbulence that had disturbed his sleep. He shivered once more as the spray from an incoming wave blew across his face. Ignoring its hard, chilly surface, Robin returned to the bottom of the boat to escape the wetness and seek shelter from the wind.

He watched his father at the front of the boat and saw the man's body tense an instant before a wave of unusual size swept across the bow. Ted Harris glanced back and smiled when he realized the building storm had awakened Robin from his sleep. Despite himself Robin returned the smile and relaxed before the impact of the next wave.

"We're not far off!" Ted shouted. "This storm's going to get a lot worse, but we'll be warm and dry before we have to worry about that. Just hold on and enjoy the ride." With a grin and a wink, his father turned back and ducked as the next wave swept in and blew over the windshield. His confidence restored, Robin looked skyward and closed his eyes to meet the fine mist of spray.

From his earliest memory, a single smile from his father could make everything in the world seem okay. He just couldn't imagine his father in a situation that was too hard to handle. When he was eight years old, back in 1953, he had seen his father in a fight. He knew that as a corporal in the Royal Canadian Mounted Police his father faced some tough situations, but he had always been protected from the reality of his father's work. It had terrified him to see his father rolling on the ground with someone who was trying to harm him.

A Dutch trapper with flaming red hair named Fritz had come in off the trap line, and after consuming a considerable quantity of homebrew, was looking for a fight with anyone. Robin had been out for a walk with his father when they heard the angry shouts of an argument in progress. In a small northern town like Fort McPherson in the

Northwest Territories, everyone knew the local RCMP constables.

When Fritz saw Robin's father, he calmed down. "Good Officer! My friend! It good see you here. We just having fun to celebrate my birthday." With a big grin on his ruddy face, Fritz held out his meaty hand.

In the split second Ted took to ease his hand forward, Fritz lunged and the two tumbled to the ground. At six feet and 185 pounds, Robin's father was lean and muscular, his size not reflecting his true strength earned from years of dog team patrol and manual labour required of a policeman in a small northern community. Fritz, however, was a good 250 pounds, with bulk that was hard to handle.

Robin stood motionless, his mind crippled with fear, his heart pounding in his ears with a deafening roar. How long he remained there he had no idea, but Rachel Reindeer happened by and gently took him by the hand.

"Don't look, Robin," she told him "You shouldn't be here. Help is on its way, so let me take you to your mother."

With a crowd now gathering, Rachel had no choice but to lead Robin past the two men where they lay grappling. As he passed, Robin glanced down, and the world seemed to slip into slow motion. Ted was on his back with Fritz on top. When Robin passed, his father looked directly into his eyes. There was blood at the corner of Ted's mouth, but his gaze made all of that fade away. Robin peered into those clear hazel eyes he had known since he was a baby. What he saw there wasn't fear, or hate, or confusion. They were calm, almost smiling, and they spoke to Robin with more clarity than any spoken words.

Go home, son, the eyes seemed to say. *I'll be fine. This silliness is almost over and I'll be along to tuck you in after a bit. I love you, son.*

Everything had been fine, and his father had come home to tuck him in. He later learned that Rachel's husband, Johnny, had arrived soon after and helped get Fritz under control. Johnny worked with Ted as a Native special constable, and though he seldom became involved in this side of their work, he was capable all the same. Robin had seen that look in his father's eyes many times since, but that fight with Fritz for some reason held a special, significant place in his memory.

Now another huge wave slammed the boat and jarred Robin's spine against the icy bottom where he sat. Once again he studied the shore to get some idea how far away they were from Fort McPherson.

With the overcast sky and a continual barrage of spray misting his eyes, spotting the usual landmarks wasn't the easiest task in the world. The Peel River was almost a mile wide in places, and no matter how much Robin squinted, images didn't always come into focus. He would have asked his father how much farther they had to go, but Ted was busy enough in the bow.

The shore of the river was covered in gravel in most places with the odd stretch of sand. Beyond the gravel shoreline, willows grew thick and dense. The banks rose sharply above this maze of branches and were covered in a blanket of dark evergreen forest. Depending on where a person went ashore, the willows could make any initial progress quite difficult.

As Robin stared at the willows through the mist and the increasingly dimming light, they appeared murky and forbidding. He imagined thousands of small yellowish diamond-shaped eyes staring back. He pictured legions of trolls crouched and ready to charge should the speed-boat venture too close. With their protruding foreheads glistening with sweat and rain, they bared their sharp teeth as they gibbered in excited anticipation.

Robin's attention wandered upward, and he followed the top edge of the bank as the boat moved past. His eyes raced ahead, and he strained to see far into the distance. The fog seemed to solidify, then he realized the darkness was actually some object at the top of the bank on the horizon. The object seemed to move, but Robin couldn't tell if his senses were being truthful or if the movement was simply a trick of poor light and intense staring.

As the boat drew closer and the object grew larger, its craggy outline sharpened and took shape. Looming high on the bank, the familiar sight of Shildii Rock told Robin they were almost home.

Shildii Rock was the subject of Gwich'in legend. Robin had heard the story many times and liked to listen as each person told his or her own version. He loved legends and imagined a time when the Native stories were real and not superstition. His mother had taught him to respect the Gwich'in beliefs — the stories, the songs, the dances.

Robin absently let his eyes follow the rock as their boat passed it. He had seen Shildii from this same vantage point many times, but the irregular shape always attracted his attention. At its base the rock was roughly ten feet square. Slab after slab of large tile-like rock formed on top of one another, reaching a height of twelve feet. Robin always fancied the rock might have been fashioned by a giant out of thin LEGO pieces haphazardly placed together in a big pile.

He watched the rock recede behind them, then turned away to look forward. It took him a moment to realize what he had just seen. Part of the rock had actually moved! He was sure of it! Not when he was staring at it in the distance, but right now as he turned away. He shouted at his father, but the wind carried any sound away and he knew it was hopeless. They were now a good piece from the rock, and all Robin could do was stare back as they moved farther and farther off. The mist and rain began to close in behind them, and the outline of Shildii Rock blurred as it receded. At that moment a figure slowly rose from where it had been crouching beside the rock, then was gone.

Robin blinked at the wall of grey that now obscured his view upriver. Had he really seen someone? He glanced at his father, peered back in the direction of Shildii Rock, then looked at his father once more. Fighting the jerking movement of the boat, Robin lurched towards the bow where his father stood struggling with the wheel.

"I saw something!" Robin yelled.

Without twisting around, Robin's father tipped his head at an angle in an effort to hear his son over the weather and motor. "You saw something?"

"I saw someone!"

Ted looked back this time and caught the expression of seriousness on his son's face. Returning his attention to the front of the boat, he continued to shout over his shoulder. "What did you see, son?"

"I saw someone by Shildii Rock. He was up top, right beside it."

Robin's father glanced back again, and this time there was no mistaking the skepticism on his face.

"Dad, I know I saw someone. It was foggy, but he was standing right beside the rock. Actually, he was crouching beside it, then he stood and stared right at us."

"It was a man? Did he wave, son? Could you see who it was?"

"It was too far away to tell who it was, but I know what I saw."

"Robin, this storm is getting worse by the minute. If you're sure you saw someone, we have to go back and see. It doesn't make sense that anyone would be up there now unless he had boat trouble or something. If that's the case, we have to help."

Robin shook his head. "I saw someone, Dad. I know I did!"

His face stiff with worry, Ted slowed their speed and carefully turned the boat. They were fighting the current now, and the storm seemed to intensify as they ploughed through the waves. Their progress was agonizingly slow as they moved back upriver. It seemed to take twice as long. As Robin squinted through the thick fog, he was sure they had gone past the rock. His father angled the boat towards shore, and the fog appeared to separate and lift as they advanced. Shildii Rock loomed above them, high on the bank. Although Robin had seen the rock only moments before, he thought it was darker now. As he gazed upward, a presence seemed to stare back.

Ted worked the boat along the shore, then turned sharply and ran them gently aground. Stepping onto the side of the boat and moving to the bow, he jumped ashore and pulled them farther up onto the gravel.

"I don't see a boat anywhere, son. It's possible someone capsized and swam ashore. If he did, he might have climbed Shildii to get high enough to attract someone's attention. Shildii kind of sticks out over the fog and catches your eye. I figured this was as good a spot as any to come ashore. Our usual trail is just over there."

Robin nodded and surveyed the rock.

"No, son, you stay here," Ted said, reading his son's mind. "We were cutting it fine before we doubled back. Now every second counts. I'll hustle up, and you stay here and hold the fort."

Robin opened his mouth to speak, but his father had already turned and was jogging along the shore towards the trail. He watched as his father slipped on the gravel, regained balance, and disappeared into the willows. Robin heard Ted's progress as he started up the trail, then all was silent.

Resigned to the fact that he had to stay behind, Robin sat in the driver's seat behind the wheel.

The mist and drizzle had changed into a steady downpour, and Robin suddenly realized he was getting very wet. Zipping his jacket up to his chin, he reached down and grabbed one of the smaller canvas tarps his father kept under the seat. He quickly shook it out to full size, spread it over his legs, and pulled it snuggly up to his chin. His face remained exposed to the rain, but he didn't really notice. His mind was captivated by thoughts of who might be at Shildii Rock. It had looked to him as if the person was hiding, not trying to get help. Why was he crouching behind the rock? Why didn't he wave? It didn't make sense.

Then it hit him. The figure was a spy! A fugitive hiding from the FBI. His dad might need backup, so he better be ready. What if the spy had lured them here to get their boat? Maybe the spy had seen his father head up the bank and planned to sneak down to steal the boat. If he did, Robin would be ready! Nobody was taking their boat! He pictured his father's boss, Inspector Limpkert, shaking his hand and presenting him with an award for bravery. The inscription would read: "Presented to Robin Harris for valour and courage in the face of danger. Our country owes him its every gratitude." His friends would all be there, and they would give him a standing ovation.

"No, please! Sit down!" he would tell them. "Thank you. Really it was nothing. It was just my duty to my country as a loyal Canadian."

Wait, what was that? Robin nervously sat upright and listened. Someone was crashing through the willows downriver. His father had taken the trail up to Shildii, and that was upriver, in the other direction.

Robin examined the boat frantically, searching for something to protect himself with. His choices were a lifejacket, a gas can, the food box, or a paddle. Some choice! Climbing out of the driver's seat, he crawled to the stern and picked up the paddle. Gripping his weapon in both hands, he knelt, his eyes level with the side so he could watch the willows.

The sounds were getting closer, and it seemed as if the person was running. There! He spotted movement! He gripped the paddle and held his breath. With one last crash, a moose broke through the trees and charged onto the gravelly shore. Stumbling to a faltering stop, the animal turned and lumbered downriver. With a sigh, Robin relaxed and let the air escape from his lungs. Just a moose!

"Unless you intend to run him down and club him to death, you should put that paddle down sometime soon."

Robin almost jumped out of his skin. His father was approaching the boat from the direction of the trail. At the sight of Robin's terror-stricken face, Ted smiled despite himself and began pushing the boat offshore. As the vessel slid into the water, the Mountie clambered onto the bow, stepped over the windshield, and headed to the stern to start the motor.

While his father checked the gas and prepared to pull-start the motor, Robin couldn't contain himself any longer. "Dad, who was up there?"

"Son, other than old Mr. Moose I didn't see a darn thing."

"But, Dad —"

"Robin, I can't really talk right now. We would've beaten this storm, but our little stop has slowed us down enough that things could get real bad. The wind is stronger, and look at the size of these waves. The wind's driven some of the fog off, but we've got a slow, rough ride ahead. If we don't leave now, we'll be up at Shildii waving for help ourselves."

The motor kicked over on the third pull. Ted moved to the bow as they slowly turned downriver. The ride was incredibly bumpy, and all Robin could do was sit on the bottom and pout. He knew he had seen someone! But it had been foggy. Could it have been the moose? No way! It was a person; the fog couldn't change things that much. His father was right, though. Why would anyone be up there in this storm, and if they needed help, they certainly wouldn't try to hide.

The rest of the trip was painful. Painfully slow in the choppy water. Painful on the butt as Robin sat on the clammy boat bottom. And painfully frustrating as he tried to figure things out. When they pulled up to the dock in Fort McPherson, it was close to midnight and Robin was happy to scramble out of the boat and into the cab of the RCMP pickup out of the rain. By the time his father secured the boat and stowed the equipment, Robin was sound asleep.

Ted hopped into the pickup cab and started the engine. As he waited for the truck to warm up, he studied the face of his sleeping son. Gently, he brushed the sandy hair away from Robin's face and touched the boy's cheek with his fingertips. The summer sun had brought out freckles that seemed to gather over his son's nose and spread across the rise of the boy's cheeks, adding an innocence to the sleeping face. He was a great kid, but what an imagination! For the most part it was kind of cute, but sometimes, like today, it seemed to get out of hand. If it was a phase, it was lasting far too long. From the time he could first speak Robin had been a storyteller. Ted smiled to himself. Maybe someday Robin would be a writer. He slipped the truck into gear and headed for home.

Chapter 2

Robin squeezed hard against the base of the rock and held his breath. Why had he come back here? Why couldn't he have left well enough alone and forgotten the whole thing? His curiosity had gotten him into trouble before, but this time it was worse than anything he had imagined. He could hear twigs snapping along the trail, and he knew it wouldn't be long before they reached him. He could try to run, but where?

Gravel skittered a few feet away to the left. Robin bit his lower lip as he tried to keep from sobbing out loud. He closed his eyes and wished the whole thing would just evaporate and go away.

It was quiet now. Too quiet. Robin opened his eyes, releasing the breath gradually from his lungs. Heart pounding, he inched his way to the side of the rock. He should stay put, but he had to take a look. Slowly, he leaned forward and stuck his head around the corner of the rock.

More gravel rattled directly behind him, and as he turned, a rough set of hands clamped around his neck ...

Robin bolted upright in bed! Just a dream! He slumped back onto the pillow and closed his eyes. It had seemed so real. He could almost smell the bush and feel the hands grabbing his neck. Unconsciously, he raised one hand to his neck and rubbed it gingerly as if it had, in fact, been bruised by the hands he had dreamt.

Shildii Rock. What had he really seen? Was it a human, or was it a trick of the mist and fog? Darn it all, there had been someone there! It wasn't as if he had seen a shadow or merely caught a brief glimpse. There had been a person there staring at him. Whoever it was hadn't wanted to be discovered and had taken off before his dad could reach the rock. Why? Why would anyone from town not want to be seen? Unless they weren't from town!

Voices from the next room broke his train of thought. His father was getting ready for work. Their house was small, but Robin had never imagined anything different. There were five rooms: his parents' bedroom, his room, the bathroom, the living room, and the kitchen. His parents' bedroom was on one side of his bedroom and the kitchen was on the other. He liked the closeness.

At night as he lay awake in bed, the low, rumbling tones of his parents' voices in their bedroom hummed through the walls and soothed him to sleep. In the morning those same voices gently eased him awake from the kitchen as his parents prepared for the day ahead.

The aroma of coffee stole under his door, and he breathed deeply as his senses came to life. He had never tasted coffee, but it sure smelled good. Robin stretched beneath the covers and enjoyed the soft warmth of their texture against his skin. He could take his time getting up, but soon school would start and the luxury of waking at his own pace would be lost. Hey! How could it slip his mind! With only a couple of days until school began that meant any families still out at summer camps would be returning to Fort McPherson. Johnny Reindeer and his family would be home any day! Johnny's son, Wayne, was Robin's best friend in the world. They had grown up together practically since birth.

Robin and Wayne had taken their first steps together and spoken their first words together. Johnny often took the two boys on the land with him, and they accompanied both Johnny and Ted on dog team patrol. They had fun together and had gotten into trouble together.

Wayne had broken his leg after Robin had convinced him that a towel flying from his neck like a cape would help him drift slowly to the ground if he jumped off the dog feed shack. Robin had received his first black eye after Wayne had persuaded him to step on the blade of a garden shovel to see just how fast the handle would fly up.

Spending so much time with Wayne and his family, Robin had actually spoken Gwich'in fluently before he mastered English. At first his parents had been concerned but soon realized it was part of growing up in their community. Fort McPherson was situated on the Peel River, just inside the Arctic Circle and south of Inuvik. The population was about 600 people. Robin and his family were three of only twenty non-aboriginal people in the community. The rest of the population were Gwich'in Dene or Métis.

Hearing the door slam as his father left for work, Robin sat up in bed. He swung his legs over the side, yawned widely, and once again stretched as hard as he could. Rubbing the sleep from his eyes, he passed over the cold tile floor to the bathroom across the hall. When he was finished in the bathroom, he returned to his bedroom to dress. The days were cooler now, so Robin slipped on a pair of corduroy pants and put on one of his warmer shirts. Still groggy, he strolled into the kitchen and plunked himself down at the table.

"Wow, somebody's up early!" Marjorie Harris said, smiling at her son as she busied herself at the stove. Robin could smell oatmeal from across the room. He laid his head on the table, placed his hands under his cheek, and stretched the last sleep from his body. His mother chuckled as she put the steaming bowl beside him and absently wove her fingers through his bed-tousled hair. Moving back to the stove, she continued with her chores.

Robin dug his spoon into the hot mixture and watched the steam rise as he moved the lumps around in the bowl. "The Reindeers got back yesterday, didn't they?"

"They did, and not much before you and your father did. That means they need their sleep." Raising her eyebrows, Marjorie glanced back at her son as she spoke.

Robin opened his mouth to speak, but his mother shook her head slowly. Knowing defeat, Robin lowered his head and went about finishing his oatmeal. As he washed down the last bite with a gulp of powdered milk, he stood to leave.

"Mind what I said, Robin."

"I will, Mom," Robin replied as he headed for the porch. "I'm just going to hang around the compound until I'm sure someone's awake over there." He slipped on a light jacket and stepped out onto the back porch. Standing in the cool air for a moment, he sat on the steps to figure out what boring thing he could do until Wayne was up.

Marjorie glanced out the kitchen window at Robin as she worked at the sink. She slowly lowered the knife she had been using to chop vegetables for supper and studied her son as he sat on the steps. He had grown over the summer. Robin was tall for twelve, and she figured he must be at least five foot four now. Although he had sprung up, he was solid for his age. He would be in grade seven this year, and it just didn't seem possible. Ted kept a running measurement of Robin's height on the doorway to his bedroom. She would have to remind him to get Robin to stand still for a moment so they could mark him off and see just how much he had grown.

Robin stared at the Richardson Mountains to the west. He could see new snow on the higher peaks, which meant it wouldn't be long before they got their first skiff of the season. Just beyond the Richardsons lay Yukon Territory. Because Fort McPherson was so close to the mountains, the weather could at times be unpredictable. One thing that was predictable, however, was that winter would soon hit with full force.

The poplars and birches had turned shades of orange and yellow. Mixed with the evergreens, the contrasts were quite startling. Although there were no trees on the Richardsons themselves, the tundra-like terrain had shifted with the season to a wonderful blend of red, burgundy, orange, and green.

The RCMP compound was located at the western edge of Fort McPherson along the bank above the Peel River. The compound itself was comprised of eight buildings. Three structures lined the most westerly bank above the river. From south to north were the staff house where the Harrises lived, the building that housed the office and single men's quarters, and Johnny Reindeer's house. Directly east of the Harris home was the jail, and beside it, just north, was the dugout icehouse at the centre of the compound. At the eastern side of the compound, towards the rest of town, also running south to north, were the dog cookhouse, dog feed shack, and the dog corral.

As he gazed across the river at the mountains, Robin's mind shifted back to Shildii Rock. What could he do to convince his father he had actually seen something? He and Wayne had to figure something out!

A cold, wet nose poking at the back of his neck startled Robin. "Dana!" He smiled as he reached back and took the dog in a gentle headlock. She licked his cheek when he scratched behind her ears. Robin stroked the big German shepherd's side, and her mouth opened in a tongue-filled doggie smile.

Dana was Ted Harris's lead dog, and the best lead dog anyone had seen. Her mother had been a show dog, but Dana was born with two floppy ears that just wouldn't stand up like a show dog's should. When Robin's mother lived down south, she had purchased Dana and brought her north. Although the German shepherd would never have the appearance to show, she had an intelligence that was seldom found in any dog.

No one had heard of a German shepherd leading a dog team of huskies, but Dana was amazing. She followed every sound of Ted's voice. Even the best lead husky could be stubborn, but not Dana. Ted would amaze people by getting Dana to lead her team to complete figure eights and other manoeuvres. The best lead huskies often hesitated at a Y in the trail and needed considerable coaxing before they would go in the right direction. With a simple "Chaw" ("Right") or "Yee" ("Left") from Ted, Dana took the correct turn every time.

Most lead dogs were male, but Dana was female. Although they often fought among themselves, the other dogs never fought with Dana and seemed to give her a special respect. While the rest of the team was post-tied in the dog corral, Dana ran free. A loose dog always sent the corrals of huskies into a barking frenzy, but not when it was Dana.

"What do you think, Dana? Am I nuts?" Dana cocked her head at an angle and gave a small snort. "Of course, I'm not nuts. I knew you would be on my side." Robin hugged the German shepherd and ruffled her fur.

"You missed me so much, you need to tell

Dana your problems?"

Robin looked up as Wayne sauntered over and plopped himself down. Wayne was Robin's age, roughly the same height, but slightly lighter in build. With jet-black hair and a dusky Gwich'in complexion that had darkened from a summer at camp in the sun, he was a distinct contrast to Robin's sandy hair and fair, freckled skin.

"Did I ever miss you!" Robin said. "These last two weeks seemed like two months!"

Wayne smiled. "Actually, it was kind of like that for me, too. Our camp's great, but after you've been out there for a while with nobody but my mom and dad and sisters, it starts to get to you a bit."

Robin nodded and glanced back at the mountains. He had been anxious to tell his friend about what he had seen, but now he wondered if even Wayne would believe him.

"Oh, man, Robin, I almost forgot. I shot my first moose. It was great!"

Robin's story would have to wait, but he didn't mind. He and Wayne had both taken their first caribou the year before, and Robin was envious that Wayne had now brought down a moose.

"It was cool. It was kind of fluky, too, but it was cool. I brought it down with one shot. My dad says I hit it just perfect, and he never saw anyone do that on their first try. But, jeez, was it a lot of work to move and butcher! It was huge!"

Robin sat back and listened. When Wayne got excited, there was no stopping him. All a guy could do was get comfortable and listen.

"The good thing is, it wasn't far from camp. We pretty much left it where it was and butchered up the meat. Man, there's a lot! I think my dad's giving you guys some. I know he took some to Grandpa last night, and the rest will last us the best part of winter. It's pretty neat because Dad didn't even get a moose this fall. The thing was big, man! Did I tell you that?" Wayne got up and raised his arms above his head. "It stood at least this high. I betcha it weighed a couple thousand pounds, too. I —"

"I betcha by tomorrow that moose will weigh 5,000 pounds." Johnny Reindeer laughed as he approached the boys. He was a handsome man with an athletic build. His eyes were the deepest brown, and they shone with a sense of humour and a love of all things amusing in life.

Robin jumped up from the steps. "Hi, Johnny!"

Johnny chuckled. "Hey there, Redbreast!" He threw his arms around both boys and gave them a squeeze. "Wait a second. Something isn't right here." Johnny took a step back and surveyed the two boys, hands on his hips. "Well, well, well. Somebody isn't the king of the hill anymore. Mr. Wayne, I hereby change your name to Shorty!"

The two boys took the first good look at each other. Johnny was right. Robin had always been a touch shorter than Wayne. There was no mistake, however. Robin now gazed down into Wayne's eyes. Robin puffed out his chest and began to laugh.

"Aw, get lost!" Wayne said, pretending he was mad. "I'm just temporarily shorter 'cause Dad kept pushing my head down in the bush trying to get me to hide from the moose."

Johnny started to laugh and slapped his knee. The two boys never ceased to amaze him. So much like brothers yet so different. Robin with his sandy hair, fair skin, and freckles. Wayne with his jet-black hair and dark complexion. Robin with his wild imagination, and Wayne the willing accomplice, so anxious to follow his friend into the middle of trouble.

"My stomach can't handle any more of this," Johnny said, holding his sides. "Wayne, I need your help now, so say goodbye. You can come back after if it's not too late."

"Aw, Dad!"

"No 'Aw, Dad.' I promised your grandma we'd drop off some more moose and fish, then we have to put the rest of the meat in the icehouse."

Robin waved halfheartedly in Wayne's direction as he followed his father back towards their house. "Well, Dana, it's just you and me again." Robin sighed. "Did I tell you how I almost had to take on a moose myself? Well, I did, and it was none of that easy stuff with a gun. All I had was a boat paddle to bring the big guy down with."

Dana flashed her knowing doggie smile and lay down at Robin's feet. All she could do was enjoy the human company and listen.

Chapter 3

When Robin woke the next morning, he could smell the fresh snow. It was the smell of a world born anew in a clean blanket of whiteness. He loved the first days of winter — crisp, not too cold, bright, and clear before the sullen darkness of winter's heart settled over the land. This early snow would melt, but it lightened Robin's spirits with thoughts of dog sled rides, and snow forts soon to be built and captured. A knock on his bedroom door, and a single sentence from his mother, replaced his excitement with dread. "Time to get up for school, Robin!"

School! Back to school. A new school year. No matter how Robin said it, he couldn't get excited. He was a good student, and though he would never admit it to Wayne, he actually enjoyed school. There was, however, one big problem. He was going into grade seven. Mr. Debark, the toughest teacher in the school, taught grade seven. That man gave more homework, more detentions, and more headaches to his students than all the other teachers put together! At least that was what all the other kids said. Wayne's sister had told the boys that anyone in Mr. Debark's class could expect to have homework every night. Now that was depressing!

From the very start it seemed as if Robin was destined to have a bad day. At breakfast he tipped his bowl of cereal into his lap and had to change not only his shirt but his new school pants, as well. Then, to make matters worse, when he stopped by to pick up Wayne on the way to school, his friend had already left. Wayne's mother had sent him to drop something off at his granny's before school. Now Robin would have no choice but to walk to school by himself.

Robin left the compound and absentmindedly wove his way through town towards school. He lifted his feet methodically and watched them fall one ahead of the other on the wooden sidewalk, which was elevated to keep shoes and boots above the dirt and gravel that became a never-ending sea of mud in the spring and fall with fresh or melting snow.

Although it was early, many people were moving about, readying themselves for winter. Most of the houses in Fort McPherson were constructed of logs. The annual fall ritual of "mudding" had begun. Throughout the warmer summer months, cracks would appear between the logs. A muddy paste was prepared in fall and administered to seal structures for warmth in winter.

River scows had to be put up and sleds were being readied for travel in the cold months ahead. Most people in Fort McPherson still used dog teams, though the Hudson's Bay store had brought in several new snowmobiles. The snowmobiles were noisy, and when the RCMP tried one last winter, Robin's father had found it unreliable. It had broken down often and needed plenty of care and attention. Even though they had to be trained and fed, dogs were far more dependable.

The musky scent of smoke carried on the light breeze, evidence of wood stoves freshly lighted to chase away the early-morning chill from the log homes as people got organized for the day. The combination of fresh snow and morning sunshine made Robin squint. The snow glistened on the ground in all directions, its tiny crystals reflecting like diamonds in the sun. Diamonds! That was it! Someone had discovered diamonds at Shildii Rock and didn't want anyone else to get close. The culprits were going to smuggle them down the Peel to the Mackenzie River and then southward. Robin and Wayne would have to stop them. It would be dangerous work, but they could handle it. Agents Harris and Reindeer with their faithful attack dog Dana. Fearlessly, they would —

"Hey, Redbreast! Robin!"

Robin looked up, unsure of where his walk had taken him. He had been staring at his feet as he trudged, deep in thoughts and dreams.

"I'm over here, son. Welcome back to earth. What planet were you on?"

Robin grinned sheepishly and strode over to where Chief John Kay stood beside the sled he was working on.

"First day of school, right?" the Gwich'in chief said.

"Yeah."

"Let's see, grade seven, Mr. Debark?"

"Yeah."

"Hmm." John Kay smiled at Robin. "I heard he eats students who get behind in their work. Just adds a bit of salt and *gulp*. All gone!"

Robin chuckled. "I bet it's true! I bet he teaches just because he hates kids so much he likes torturing them every chance he can get. Being a teacher is perfect for his evil plan!"

The chief shook his head and laughed. "You sure never change, Robin. Old Mr. Debark isn't that bad. He can be a bit crusty around the edges, but his students seem to learn a lot."

"Crusty! If he was a pie, he would be all crust and no filling!"

"Well, I think you're going to find out just how crusty old Mr. Debark can be, son. It's five after nine."

Robin glanced at his watch. "Darn! See you, Chief!"

John Kay watched as Robin ran off towards the school. Smiling to himself, he turned back to the sled runner he was working on. He really needed a new one. Maybe he should buy one of those new-fangled snowmobiles they had at the Hudson's Bay store. No, things weren't that bad. Besides, those crazy machines would never replace dogs. Who would give up their dogs for the smell of gas and oil and all of that noise to go along with it?

The halls were empty when Robin arrived at the school. Every step echoed as he headed for the office to retrieve a late slip before he continued on to class. "Late, late, late, late," each step seemed to say. After reporting to the secretary, he waited at the counter as she filled in the particulars.

"Hey, Robin!" Frank Firth entered the office and slumped into one of the cushioned chairs in the waiting area.

The secretary sighed. "Oh, Frank, not already!"

Frank shrugged and smiled. One of the older students who was in grade twelve, he was a smart, funny guy. Robin had never seen him without a smile and thought he was pretty neat. The teachers didn't always appreciate Frank's humour, however, and he was always in trouble.

As Robin took the late slip from the secretary

and walked out, Frank gave him a friendly poke in the arm and a wink. "Don't worry, Robin. His Debark is worse than his Debite."

Quite pleased with his own joke, Frank giggled, and despite himself, so did Robin. *Maybe this won't be so bad,* he thought. *Maybe Mr. Debark is a nice guy just like Chief Kay said.*

Robin opened the classroom door, and as his eyes met those of Mr. Debark, he felt himself shrink and melt into the floor. The teacher's eyes were pale blue like a husky's. They bore right into a person, were impossible to read, and were colder than an icy February night. To Robin those eyes had the blank gaze of a shark just before it rolled onto its back to attack. They held the threat of a cobra's eyes as it swayed back and forth before it struck. Or maybe they were more like the eyes of a vulture as it waited for the first opportunity to rip every morsel of meat from its victim's bones.

Mr. Debark was a tall man, six foot four or five. At age fifty-eight he was slightly stooped, but that only added to his commanding presence. With his white shock of hair and elegantly hooked nose, his vulture-like form towered over Robin and dominated the class. And those pale blue eyes! A shiver rippled through Robin as he lowered his gaze and studied his feet.

"Mr. Harris, I presume?"

"Yes, sir."

"I'm glad to see you so anxious to honour us with your presence. You have a late slip, I presume?"

"Yes, sir." Without looking directly at Mr. Debark, Robin stepped forward and handed the now-crumpled paper to his teacher. He levelled his gaze on Mr. Debark's hand as it darted forward and plucked the note from his fingers.

Talons retracting, the vulture spoke. "Find your seat, Mr. Harris."

Robin quickly scanned the room, hoping to locate a seat near Wayne. The only vacant desk, however, was in the front row, next to the only face Robin didn't recognize. As he moved to sit down, he caught Wayne's eye at the far side of the room. He smiled and shrugged at Robin, helpless to communicate with his friend in any other fashion.

The silent exchange wasn't lost on Mr. Debark. He made a mental note of the alliance between the two friends. These first few days were important ones. Getting to know the students, their friendships, their motivations. There were many sides to successful learning, and all of these had to be explored if each student was to achieve his or her full potential in grade seven.

Robin settled into his seat and tried to move the contents of his backpack into the desk with the least noise possible. Mr. Debark was giving an overview of the subjects they would cover throughout the year and his rules of the classroom. Robin tried to listen and unpack at the same time. He knew everyone in the room. They had been at school together since kindergarten. There was only one class for each grade, so you always stayed with your friends from year to year. He didn't know the student sitting next to him, though.

As Mr. Debark spoke, Robin cast a sidelong glance at the new student, and when the stranger's eyes met his, Robin smiled. The boy scowled, however, and quickly trained his eyes on the blackboard at the front of the class. He was slightly shorter than Robin, with whitish-blond hair cropped short, and very pale skin. The boy had a thin but athletic build and actually looked a little imposing. Remembering that his father had mentioned that the Hudson's Bay store had a new manager coming to town and that the man had a son about Robin's age, Robin decided to shrug the scowl off as the stranger's first-day jitters and turned his attention back to Mr. Debark.

"Grade seven is what we call a transition year. You're no longer primary school students. You're officially in junior high. With this distinction comes a new responsibility and a new requirement for maturity. You'll have homework. You'll have more homework than you've experienced in the primary grades. Math, science, English, and social studies will form the core of your curriculum. We'll also have lessons in history and current events."

Mr. Debark paused. As he walked across the front of the classroom, he clasped his hands behind his back and seemed to consider at length his next words. "All homework must be top-quality and must be handed in on time. Mr. Harris, would you please come to the board and write what I just said? Mr. Harris!"

Robin jumped in his seat. His father was Mr. Harris and he wasn't used to being called that. Rising from his desk, he walked reluctantly to the front and took the chalk from Mr. Debark's hand, then stepped to the blackboard and slowly wrote: "All homework must be top-quality and must be handed in on time."

"Very good, Mr. Harris." Mr. Debark held out a hand for the chalk as Robin returned to his seat. "I trust, Mr. Harris, that you'll also remember to attend school on time."

As Robin sat down, he heard a soft chuckle. When he glanced over, the new boy had a big smirk on his face and seemed to be enjoying the attention Mr. Debark was giving Robin. What was with this guy!

Recess couldn't come soon enough. The ground in the school field had become slick and muddy from the melting snow, but Robin could have cared less. It was a break from the vulture

Debark and a chance to visit with his friends. Having headed out of the classroom at opposite ends, Robin met Wayne at the side exit and they went outside.

"I hate the first day of school," Wayne moaned.

"Me, too," Robin said. "And with this muddy ground we can't play soccer or anything."

Wayne dug into his pocket and smiled. "I brought my softball. Let's play catch. Billy!" Wayne waved at Billy Vittrekwa and motioned him over to join them. They formed a triangle and began to play barehanded catch.

The boys played in silence, happy to be in one another's company after the seemingly long summer apart, and with each toss the game fell into a comfortable rhythm without thought or effort. It was a simple game, one shared by friends the world over. A game without complex rules or a need to win. A game to be played in comfortable silence or with casual talk between friends.

"Mr. Debark's something else!" Wayne said eventually.

Robin sighed. "That's the understatement of the century!"

Billy snorted. "You missed half of it. You were at least fifteen minutes late. We got the whole rundown on his dos and don'ts. 'Well, Mr. Vittrekwa, my expectations for you are extremely high. Grade seven is what we call a transition year. You're officially in junior high. With this distinction comes added responsibility and a requirement for maturity with proper deportment.' What the heck is deportment?"

"Stop it, Billy," Robin pleaded. "You're starting to scare me."

The boys laughed as they continued to toss the ball.

"And what's up with that new kid?" Robin asked. "Has he ever got an attitude. You should have seen him laughing when Debark made me write on the blackboard."

"We were all laughing," Wayne teased.

"Yeah, you bet we were," Billy chimed in.

"Okay, okay," Robin said. "So you all laughed. That's not my point. That new kid just seemed snotty, that's all. I tried to be nice and he actually sneered at me."

Wayne nodded. "We know what you mean. Before you got here, we all had to introduce ourselves. It seemed kind of silly really, because we all know each other, but I guess it was for Debark and the new guy. Billy says he's Billy, Betty says she's Betty, Tommy says he's Tommy, blah, blah, blah. Then the new guy stands and says, 'My name is Timothy Parch. Not Tim or Timmy. The proper form is Timothy.'" Wayne cocked his head to one side, hands on his hips as he held the ball and continued in a high-pitched, stiff voice. "'I am from Winnipeg, which is the capital of Manitoba. It is a much more civilized place with many things to see and do.' The whole while the guy's saying all this he has this prissy look on his face and he kind of wrinkles his nose like there's a bad smell in the room or something."

"Wayne, would you please just throw the ball!" Billy pleaded.

"Why, of course, I will, my uncivilized savage friend," Wayne said in Timothy Parch's voice. He turned to the side and kicked his leg in an exaggerated manner before he followed through and released the ball. It floated high and sailed well over Robin's head. The boys watched as it landed and bounced past the monkey bars. It took one final high hop and skipped off the bottom step of the slide before it slowed to a stop not two feet from where the new boy stood.

"Oh, brother!" Billy said under his breath.

As the three friends watched, the new boy stepped carefully over to the ball. He glanced across at the boys, then looked at the ball and gave it a tentative nudge with his toe.

"Hey, Timothy!" Wayne yelled. "Throw it back!"

The boy flinched, seemingly surprised at the sound of his own name. But his alarmed expression quickly shifted to a look of something closer to anger. Turning away, he stomped on the ball and continued his walk towards the school.

Wayne kicked at the ground. "What the heck was that? I don't believe it."

"I told you," Robin said. "The guy seems mad about everything. You laughed when I said he sneered at me, but did you see that look on his face?"

Billy ambled over and gingerly plucked the ball out of the sticky gumbo where it had been squashed. Shaking his head, he wiped the ball on his pants as Robin and Wayne moved over to join him. "If that guy doesn't smarten up, I might have to give him a good shot to the old melon," Billy mumbled, still examining the ball as if it had been permanently damaged.

"That won't help anything, Billy, and we all know it," Robin said. "Maybe the guy's confused with moving here from Winnipeg and all. We just need to give him a chance."

At the moment the bell sounded, signalling the end of recess and the boys' discussion.

"I don't know, Robin," Wayne said as they trudged back to the school. "There's confused and there's just plain rude." Wayne put his arm around his friend's shoulder as they reached the school steps. "Whatever his problem is, I hope he gets over it soon or he won't be making many friends here."

The rest of the day didn't allow for much more thought about Timothy Parch. Mr. Debark jumped into a detailed math lesson followed by the introduction of a new novel study. The torture had begun!

Whenever Robin had to pass a handout to the new boy, he accepted it without even glancing at it. Robin thought he actually might get the chance to say something to Timothy, but at the end of class the new boy hurriedly collected his books and rushed out ahead of the other students.

Robin met Wayne at the door, and they passed into the crowded hall. Manoeuvring through the sea of familiar faces, they exchanged the odd friendly poke with friends they hadn't seen since the previous school year. The air outside had cooled once more, and the muddy ground was beginning to thicken with the drop in temperature.

"My dad says freeze-up's going to come real quick this year," Wayne said. "He figures lots of snow, too. I can't wait. I hate this muddy stuff."

Robin nodded. "Me, too. I know my dad's going to let me drive the dog team a lot more this year. He says he might even let me run Dana in the New Year's race."

"That would be terrific. Nobody can touch you and Dana. Danny Francis might get a big surprise. His three years of being undefeated might just come to an end."

The boys grinned at each other and continued walking towards the compound.

"Wayne, is your dad keeping his nets in the water for a while?"

"Yeah, I actually think he went out and checked for fish today. Why?"

"No big reason," Robin said, trying to be nonchalant. "I was kind of hoping to catch a ride with him and spend some time up at Shildii Rock while he's upriver. He could pick me up on the way back. You'd come with me, of course," he quickly added, reading his friend's mind.

Wayne raised an eyebrow. "Shildii Rock? Why the sudden interest in it? Are we going to have a little picnic or something?"

"Nothing like that. I … I was going to tell you yesterday, but you were telling me about your moose and you were pretty busy and stuff. I … well, I saw something — someone — up there the other day and I have this funny feeling about it."

"Here we go! Was it a runaway from the French Foreign Legion this time, or just a fugitive axe murderer? Or maybe a zombie? I don't know if I'm ready to tackle another one of those."

Robin smiled sheepishly. "I'm not sure what, or who, I saw, but I saw someone." He then told Wayne about the evening boat ride on the Peel.

"That does kind of sound weird, Robin. I believe you saw someone, but I sure can't figure out why they'd be up there, either." The two walked on in silence for a bit, then Wayne stopped and turned to Robin. "Tell you what. I'll ask Dad if we can head out with him on Saturday. I know he's planning on going out again if the weather's decent."

Robin slapped his friend on the back. "I knew I

could count on you, Wayne. You're the best!"

"I'm the best, all right," Wayne said, shaking his head. "I just wonder how much trouble you're going to get me into this time."

Robin frowned as if his feelings had been hurt.

"Don't give me that look," Wayne protested. "You know what I'm talking about." When the boys approached Wayne's house, Wayne added, "See you tomorrow. And don't forget to do your homework — five pages of math and the first two chapters of *A Tale of Two Cities*."

Robin shook his head as he passed the compound office building. Why did Wayne have to remind him about the wonderful evening of homework that awaited him? If he could survive this year with Mr. Debark, he could survive anything!

Chapter 4

The temperature continued to drop over the next few days. Robin worried that things might cool off too quickly. If the river started to freeze, the trip to Shildii Rock would be delayed. Instead of heading upriver with Johnny in a boat, they would have to wait for enough ice and snow to travel by dog team.

The boys fell into the routine of school and the homework given by Mr. Debark. It was never-ending! Robin had the feeling that Mr. Debark made things harder for him than the other students. His answers never seemed quite good enough and his written assignments could always be improved upon. It was going to be one of the longest school years of his life.

Part of Robin's daily routine were the chores his parents gave him. In the summer Robin actually enjoyed most of his chores: feeding the dogs, helping his mother tend their small northern garden, going on boat patrol with his father to summer camps along the river, and helping his father or Johnny check nets for fish. It was nice to be outside in the sun and it made the work feel enjoyable. With twenty-four hours of daylight at the height of summer, everyone took advantage of the long, warm days, staying up when they pleased and sleeping when rest was needed.

During the summer, water for drinking and washing was delivered by a truck and poured into a square steel tank that was in a rough dirt basement under their small house. A crude pressure system brought the water to their living quarters. In winter it wasn't quite that easy. Ted Harris cut large blocks of ice from the Peel River. The blocks were then brought up and stored beside their house. As water was needed, blocks of ice were sent down into the metal tank through a wooden chute that extended out the side of the house. Robin helped his father with the ice, and it was heavy work. He wasn't strong enough to move blocks on his own, so he lent a hand with the tools and shifted ice down the chute. This was more important when his father was out of town on patrol and his mother needed assistance.

There was one chore that Robin was responsible for year-round — looking after the honey bucket. What a job! Nobody had a flush toilet in Fort McPherson. They either had an outhouse or a honey bucket. An outhouse was okay, but at minus forty degrees it was kind of nasty wading through snow and wind to end up freezing in a wooden closet.

The honey bucket really was a bucket. It had a toilet seat and a cover around it. In the Harris bathroom a galvanized steel pipe went from the back of the cover and outside to help vent the smell. A garbage bag was placed inside the bucket and folded over the top under the seat. People did their business in the garbage bag in the honey bucket. At the end of the day the bucket was carried out and the garbage bag was tied off and disposed of.

It was this wonderful task that Robin presided over. He had learned the hard way that no matter how tempting, it wasn't a chore you put off too long. If the bag got too full, the bucket became real heavy, and nobody wanted a full honey bucket slopping its contents all over. A person risked his life if he tried to lift a bag that was too full and it went *sploosh!*

The garbage bags were placed beside the road and picked up by a truck throughout the week. Sometimes a storm came up and the bags were buried before they could be taken away. In springtime when the sun came out and the snow melted, the odd "honey bag" began to show itself. The boys then played the dangerous game of "I dare you to jump on the honey bag." If the bag was still mostly frozen and you jumped on it, you were safe. If the bag had melted, you found yourself covered in the contents with a sickening splash. Robin had lost at this game only once and had never played again. His bottom still remembered the spanking he had received from his father when he returned home covered in "stuff."

Timothy Parch didn't seem to be getting over his "confusion" caused by moving to Fort McPherson. He ignored the rest of the class when they were in school, and they never saw him once the day was over. Robin's father said that this was because Timothy's father made him help out at home. He didn't have a mother, so his after-school chores at home and in the store were very heavy.

The nicest thing about the cold fall weather was the new jacket that Wayne's mom had sewn for Robin. It was a fancy traditional one made from caribou. Mrs. Reindeer had created designs on the back with red, green, and blue beads. Wayne had a similar jacket, and the two boys proudly wore them to school each day.

Robin knew how much work it took to tan the caribou hide, let alone do the beadwork. When a caribou was killed, it was skinned and the meat was eaten. The women first plucked off the skin's long hair, then began scraping off any remaining fat or flesh. A smooth, sharp caribou bone was used for the scraping process. The caribou was stretched on a wooden frame to make the scraping easier. A special mash of caribou brain and a little water was cooked until well mixed. The freshly scraped hide was then soaked in the brain mash overnight. This process of stretching and soaking was repeated several times until the hide was soft. Dry, rotten willow branches were gathered as fuel to smoke the hide. Only after all this work was done was the hide ready for clothing or other purposes. To receive a gift such as this new jacket, which had taken such care and effort to make, was very special indeed.

By Saturday the weather had consistently shifted to temperatures below zero. The smell of snow was strong in the air as they readied themselves for the journey upriver. Johnny told the boys that this was likely the last trip he would make to the nets before freeze-up.

A light cover of snow had remained on the ground for several days, and the sullen grey morning promised more to come. Although the Reindeers' summer camp was about four miles downriver on the Peel, Johnny also kept a net upriver past Shildii Rock in the fall. It was Johnny's job to catch fish to feed the RCMP dogs, and he gathered as much as possible before winter. His one net wasn't enough and other sources of fish were necessary.

Special Constable André Jerome lived in the community of Tsiigehtchic, which was located where the Arctic Red River and the Mackenzie River met. Every fall Johnny travelled north on the Peel River and on into the Mackenzie River near Point Separation. From there it was a short trip on the Mackenzie to Tsiigehtchic.

Johnny usually fished with André and brought a huge load of fish back to be put up for the dog teams. Today, however, the trip would be a short one upriver a couple of miles past Shildii Rock. Johnny would drop the boys off and pick them up on the way back.

The trip would be somewhat slow, since Johnny used the RCMP twenty-two-foot freighter canoe to check the nets. It was a great craft for hauling fish, but with its ten-horsepower engine it chugged along at a much slower pace than the speedboat.

Robin and Wayne settled near the bow as Johnny started them upriver. There was a breeze and it was extremely cold. Robin pulled the collar of his jacket over his mouth and blew warm air inside as he huddled beside Wayne. If he stayed perfectly still, he didn't shiver. His mind raced ahead to what they might find at Shildii Rock.

Someone had been there who didn't want to be seen. Why? Because he was trying to hide something? What? He was a criminal! He must be wanted for something. Murder! Maybe he was on that "Most Wanted" poster that hung on the wall in his father's office. It could be dangerous, but he and Wayne could handle it. They would have to be careful. A trap. Yes, that was it. They would have to set some kind of trap to catch this fugitive from the law.

An elbow to the ribs snapped Robin back to reality. Wayne pointed at the riverbank and Shildii Rock above. Robin watched as Johnny turned the freighter towards shore. The rock stood tall and barren, outlined by the grey sky. Robin had seen it so many times, but only now took notice of how irregular its outline really was. Maybe the legend about Shildii was true. In fact, maybe what Robin had seen was a ghost of Gwich'in magic and not a real person.

Johnny moved the freighter into shore and steadied the craft so the boys could jump out. "I won't be at the nets for long guys, so pay attention to the time. It's ten o'clock now, and I shouldn't be back any later than 11:30." The boys nodded and pushed Johnny back out into the current. "And, hey!"

Robin and Wayne looked back.

"Whatever you two are up to, stay out of trouble!" Johnny smiled, and with a wave he was off upriver. The boys turned and hiked up the trail in silence.

"You know, Wayne, sometimes it scares me how well your dad knows the two of us," Robin finally said.

Wayne nodded. "Yeah, well, you try living

with that every day. It's really hard to get away with anything."

The climb up to Shildii was steep, and the boys didn't have much time. Although the day was dull, the crisp, cool air that was just below freezing gave it freshness and life. Once the trail wound through the willows that grew along the shore, it rose sharply and passed through a maze of scrawny evergreens. The brush grew thin here and visibility was good. The boys didn't stop until they reached the top of the bank, where they paused to catch their breath. The ground was covered with loose shale that clattered underfoot as they walked.

Behind Shildii Rock, away from the river and to the west, the trees were thicker. Robin saw rolling hills in the distance. Somewhere beyond those hills lay Alaska, and farther south, not many miles away, was Yukon Territory.

The boys stood next to Shildii Rock, not quite sure of what to do next. Robin stared up at the rock and tried to imagine all the different people who had stood in this exact spot. "What did you see?" he whispered. "Who was here? I need to know." He placed a hand on the rock, almost expecting to feel vibration or movement in answer to his question.

Wayne shook his head. "Now you're talking to a rock. There's a family of trees over here who saw the whole thing. Maybe you should ask them a question or two."

Robin smiled. "I know, I know. Your dad's going to be back right away, so let's start looking."

"What exactly are we looking for?"

"I don't know. Anything that looks out of place, I guess. A footprint, a piece of paper, maybe gun shells or something. Anything that shouldn't be here."

Wayne nodded and moved west, away from the bank, while Robin walked south along the bank, past the trail they had followed up from the river.

What were they looking for? Robin wondered. A phantom that maybe he hadn't really seen? If someone had been here, he certainly wouldn't stick around. But Robin had seen someone, and he knew it! He had to stop questioning himself and prove it.

Most of the snow had either melted or blown clear at the top of the bank. If some snow had remained on the ground, there might still be footprints. Robin wandered along the edge and turned inland to work his way back towards the rock. He surveyed the distant hills. Somewhere out there was Alaska, the most northerly part of the United States. Wait a minute! If a Soviet spy wanted to sneak into the United States, he could do it through Alaska! Robin halted as his mind continued to wander. A Soviet spy plane could fly across undetected, parachute a spy into the

Northwest Territories near Fort McPherson, and get away without being spotted.

The United States and Canada had men stationed roughly every forty miles along the Arctic Ocean coast, but there were none this far south. The sites where the men were stationed formed part of what was called the Distant Early Warning or DEW Line. One of the main stations was northeast in Tuktoyaktuk on the Arctic coast. If a Soviet spy plane had slipped through and parachuted a man in, it would be up to Wayne and Robin to stop him! He would be dangerous; Soviet spies always were. He would be armed with a Russian-issue revolver and would be highly trained. But he wouldn't be trained well enough! Wayne and Robin were RCMP special agents, and nothing was tricky enough to fool them.

"Hey, Robin!" Wayne called out.

Snapping back to his senses, Robin shouted, "Over here, Wayne!" He didn't know how long he had been standing there and he tried to look alert as his friend approached.

"I looked all over the place, Robin, but I couldn't spot a thing. Did you have any luck?"

"Well, I started near the bank, and when you shouted I was just going to —"

"Call me over to see this trail! Wow, it never used to be here! Somebody must be coming here from the west. It kind of curls off into the trees."

Robin nodded absently as he followed Wayne's eyes and spotted the narrow trail in front of him. How had he missed it? It was right where he had been standing, deep in his daydreams. "You know, to be honest, Wayne, I never really —"

"Let's follow it!"

Robin nodded and fell behind Wayne as he moved along the trail. Wayne was right. Robin had been up to Shildii a lot over the summer, and this trail had never been here. He felt his heart racing as he shadowed Wayne into the bush.

They both heard the sound at the same time. Wayne stopped and glanced at Robin. As the sound grew louder, they both knew exactly what it meant.

"Not now!" Wayne sighed. "Why does Dad have to come back right now?"

The boys knew they were defeated. Johnny had told them to head to the shore and be ready to leave when he returned.

"Let's not tell anybody about this, Wayne."

"Why not?"

"They won't believe us, or they'll have some explanation. It's our secret now and let's keep it that way. Once freeze-up's over, we can bring Dana and the team out here for a run. If someone's really using this trail, the snow will be packed and we'll see it. If it's not packed, we'll know it's nothing."

Wayne studied his friend, trying to judge how

much trouble this could get them into. Finally, he nodded. "Okay, but let's get down to the river before my dad gets there."

Robin began to run towards Shildii Rock and the trail down to the river. As he neared the rock, he heard a yelp. Glancing back, he saw that Wayne had taken a tumble while trying to catch up. "You okay, Wayne?" he shouted.

Wayne nodded as he pushed himself to his knees. He stared at his hands, Robin guessed, to inspect the scrapes and cuts he had received from his fall on the sharp shale. Finally, Wayne gathered himself, rose to his feet, and continued after Robin.

The boys half ran, half slid down the trail, and as they burst through the willows onto the gravel shore, they spied Johnny standing by the freighter canoe at the water's edge. Johnny laughed as the boys exploded through the willows and skidded to a stop like two comedians rushing frantically into a scene in a slapstick movie. "So what did you two super sleuths find?"

"We didn't find anything, Dad," Wayne said, making his best attempt to sound disappointed.

"That's too bad, boys." Johnny smiled and ruffled Robin's hair. "The bad guys must have known it was you two coming and skedaddled. Sometimes I feel like running away, too, when I see you boys coming, and I'm not even a criminal."

"Stop it, Dad," Wayne said quietly, feeling guilty about lying to his father.

The boys walked to the boat with Johnny and jumped aboard as he pushed off. The motor flipped over with a single pull, and Johnny swung them out into the current. The water was smooth, and the boys settled near the bow as Johnny steered from the stern.

The fresh air had taken its toll, and Robin closed his heavy eyes against the wind. He felt the light-headedness of fast-approaching sleep and slumped onto the bottom of the boat, trying to get as comfortable as possible. A slight nudge from Wayne roused him, and he turned to give his friend a look of frustration at being disturbed so close to a comfortable sleep. He felt Wayne's hand touch his and he opened his fingers as Wayne passed something across.

Forgetting his annoyance, Robin placed his closed fist in his lap. Slowly, he opened his fingers and stared at a blue piece of paper in his palm. He turned the paper over and peered at the white lettering spread across its surface. The paper was actually a book of matches. Finding a book of matches was unusual in itself. Everybody used boxes of wooden matches around Fort McPherson, and Robin had only seen cardboard matches once before in his life. Even more unusual was what the writing said across the blue cardboard cover: "High Top Bar,

Billings, Montana." Any type of paper that fell to the ground and remained outside for even a short time would weather and fade. The bright blue surface of this book of matches shone up at Robin, crisp and new.

Chapter 5

Every spare moment the boys had together, they talked about the book of matches Wayne had found and what its presence at Shildii Rock meant. The boys had many ideas, but none they were certain about. They did, however, decide not to tell their parents. Both of them felt guilty about the deception, but agreed that this was one mystery they needed to solve on their own. In the past they had come up with some pretty bizarre ideas and ways of getting into trouble. They needed to prove something wasn't right before anyone else was told.

Mr. Debark was puzzled by the boys' sudden interest in geography, specifically Montana and that portion of the United States. However, he gladly showed them where it was located along the southern border of Canada and gave them some history on the early settlement of the area.

The West! The Wild West! Robin couldn't help himself. His mind went crazy with the idea —

cowboys, outlaws, sheriffs! An outlaw wanted for rustling cattle and the murder of a rancher had stolen into Canada across the border. Where would be the best place to hide if you didn't want anyone to find you? The Canadian North, of course. No sheriff was going to hunt for an outlaw all the way to the Arctic Circle. There was no doubt about it. He and Wayne had to form a posse of two and round this critter up. Dana was a little too small to ride, but along with the other dogs and sled they would have their own stagecoach. It would be great! Yee-haw!

Freeze-up was well underway, and soon there would be enough snow and ice to make travel by dog team safe. As the weeks wore on, the boys' minds shifted to thoughts of Christmas, dog team races, and the camping trips with their fathers that lay ahead.

School had taken a turn for the worse, though. Mr. Debark didn't like anything Robin did. There was always some little or big thing, depending on the situation, that Robin supposedly did wrong. On top of all that, Timothy Parch could do no wrong. The new boy was as stuck-up as ever, and every time Mr. Debark told the class how well Timothy did on an assignment, Timothy rubbed it in with a sneaky little smile or a knowing glance in Robin's direction.

Robin tried his best to stay friendly, and even though he sometimes boiled with anger, he always said "Hi" when he passed Timothy in the hall or somewhere around town. To win Timothy over, he even took the blame for a disaster the kid caused in science.

The class was attempting to fashion miniature volcanoes with vinegar and baking soda. Timothy somehow spilled vinegar into the main mixture before Mr. Debark distributed it to each student. The single "huge" volcano that was created was quite the sight and also made quite the mess. Robin happened to be standing beside the explosion as Timothy calmly walked away. When confronted by Mr. Debark, Robin didn't try to shift the responsibility. He simply accepted the two-week detention and remained quiet. Timothy, for his part, kept silent, too. His only acknowledgement of the situation was his usual smug grin and detached presence at the desk next to Robin.

But it was now winter, and Robin was happy for the clean, fresh smells of the season. Most of all he was anxious for the trips with his father on the dog team and the big race that in his mind he had already won. Caring for the dogs was hard work, but to Robin it was worth it.

Feeding the dogs took preparation. They were work dogs, and proper nutrition was an important part of their everyday life. The feed shack was stocked with miracle meal, beef tallow, stick fish, and dry fish. The bags of miracle meal and boxes of beef tallow were ordered in from the south and arrived on a barge by river in the fall. Stick fish were prepared with fish harvested in the fall from the Peel and Mackenzie rivers. The dead fish were stuck on three-foot-long sticks that were cut for that purpose. The stick was poked through the gills of the fish. As many fish as possible were placed on the stick in this fashion. When the stick was full, it was hung to dry in the sun. The fish were intact with their heads and weren't gutted. Once the sun dried the skin into a hard texture, the fish were transported from the fishing camps to the feed shack in Fort McPherson for the winter.

Dry fish could be used for human or dog consumption. These fish were filleted and hung to dry. The fish that were to be used for the dogs were gathered in fifty-pound bales and were also stored in the feed shack.

When the dogs were in town and living in their pen, their meals were prepared in the cook shack. A mixture of miracle meal, stick fish, and beef tallow was prepared and placed in a huge black cauldron in the cook shack. The cauldron sat on a wood stove, and the stew-like meal was cooked as dog feed. In winter a portion of this feed was given to each dog once a day.

On the trail the dogs' meals were much simpler. Every evening each dog was given one dried fish and one-third pound of beef tallow. This type of meal gave them the energy they needed for each day on the trail.

When Ted Harris announced they would make their first dog team patrol of the season to Tsiigehtchic, Robin was ecstatic. They would leave on Saturday morning and return by Sunday evening. When his father told him that Wayne and Johnny would be coming, as well, Robin was pleased beyond words.

He woke early Saturday morning and joined his father, Johnny, and Wayne at the dog corral to prepare for the trip. They usually kept fourteen to twenty dogs, and today they all seemed to bark at the same time as Robin and the others got the toboggans ready. Robin and his father would take the main team, while Johnny and Wayne would take another. A team usually consisted of six to seven dogs. Both Ted and Johnny preferred seven dogs for the extra pulling power.

Robin and Ted's team chose Dana as lead dog, followed by Captain, Louie, Colonel, Corp, and Sarg, with Brig as wheel dog. Wayne and Johnny picked Duke for lead, followed by Springer, Staff, Mutt, Dan, and Soup, with Tag as wheel. Lead and wheel dogs were very important. The lead dog had to be smart and able to follow directions to the letter. The wheel dog needed to be strong since the pulling was hardest near the toboggan. It was also dangerous. If the toboggan was going too fast or going downhill, the wheel dog could be crushed. Brig was a smart veteran of the trail. His strength and quickness at moving aside had often saved him when the toboggan didn't stop soon enough.

The toboggans were made of two eight-foot-long oak boards. They were wide and curled high at the front. The carryall, a type of long canvas bag, was secured to the sled with thin nylon rope. The bag was narrow at the front and wide at the back. A flat wooden board with two handles at the top called a lazy-back was fastened upright about a foot from the rear of the toboggan. The carryall was fastened to the lazy-back, which pulled it up at the sides, allowing provisions and a passenger or two to ride inside. The musher stood at the back and held on to the handles. There was a metal hinge shaped like a claw at the very back that the musher pressed down into the snow with his foot to act as a brake if needed.

The dogs were secured to the front of the sled with leather traces, which were attached to leather collars that went around the dogs' necks. The traces also had back and belly pads that fitted around the dogs.

A head rope was attached to the front of the toboggan. When the toboggan was in motion, the head rope was flipped over the toboggan so that it dragged behind on the trail. If a musher fell off, he could grab the rope.

When hitching dogs, the head rope was tied to a post to prevent the dogs from racing away with the sled in their excitement. Most mushers fastened the head rope and then started hitching the dogs, beginning with the wheel position. With Dana at lead, though, Ted started with her first. She would calmly sit and maintain control as the rest of the team was put into position behind her.

Robin and Wayne loaded the toboggans with provisions as their fathers hitched the teams. After the loading was finished, the dogs stood ready, excitedly tugging at their traces, and the boys climbed into their respective fathers' toboggans. With a shout of "Okay," Johnny's team lunged ahead and set out down the main trail through town from the compound. Dana stood ready but didn't follow. She looked back at Ted, shivering in anticipation. With a nod from her master and a shout of "Okay," she turned and strained against her traces. Brig pulled hard and the team gained speed quickly.

The two teams moved through Fort McPherson in the early-morning darkness and headed southeast into the bush. From his seat in the toboggan Robin could see Johnny's back outlined against the brightening eastern sky as he led the way along the trail. Robin nestled among the rations and blankets, enjoying the sensations of the early day: the canvas smell of the carryall, the leather of the traces, the smoky caribou scent of their clothing, the clean freshness of the morning air and snow. It was minus twenty-one degrees with only a whisper of wind, perfect for travel. The sun was rising in the east ahead of them, and with it came the oranges and reds created by winter light. Their days were much shorter now, and as they moved through December their hours of brightness would continue to diminish. At the darkest of winter's heart the only light they would see would last from 11:00 a.m. to 1:00 p.m., and even that light wouldn't be at its strongest.

As they travelled farther east, the trail remained good. When they crossed the first few lakes of their journey, the trail faded. The land was flat and the growth wasn't overly dense. They would cross thirty-two lakes in total on their journey to Tsiigehtchic, all frozen and sleeping beneath winter's blanket of snow. At the sixth lake Johnny slowed his team to a stop and walked ahead to the toboggan. It was only when Robin saw Johnny remove his snowshoes from the toboggan and fasten them to his mukluks that he remembered they would have to break trail. They were the first to make the trip to Tsiigehtchic this winter, and the trail was still covered with deep, fluffy snow. Johnny and Ted would have to take turns running ahead of the dogs in their snowshoes to pack the deep snow. When the trail was good, the trip took seven hours. In these conditions, though, a tiring ten-hour trip could be expected.

Wayne took his father's place at the back of the sled as Johnny led the procession of dog teams on snowshoe. It was full daylight now. Sun and snow created a world so bright it was hard to believe there could ever be darkness. Small groups of ptarmigan sat near the trail happily feeding on willows. The birds seldom flew off as the toboggans passed, oblivious to any danger that could befall them. They looked comical with their seemingly oversize feet fluffed large with winter feathers as they stroked their beaks against the lowest willow branches. The snow was pocked with tracks, and Robin tried to name each grouping for his father — mostly caribou, fox and, unusually, one set of wolverine.

Robin took control of the sled when Ted donned his snowshoes to take a turn breaking trail. It was slow going, but Robin enjoyed the chance to stand in control, shifting his weight as the dogs turned. With Dana at lead, Robin didn't really need to give directions. Wayne and Johnny, however, had to deal with their more inexperienced dogs from time to time. Duke was a young lead dog and didn't always go in the right direction. Dan was an older, stubborn dog who could be frustrating and single-minded at the best of times.

"Yee!" Johnny shouted as Ted broke trail to the

left. "Chaw" was used by most dog mushers to move the animals to the right. Stop and go were simply "Whoa" and "Okay."

By early afternoon, they reached the midpoint of their trip. The RCMP had built a log cabin there to give travellers shelter and provide a stopover point when required. Johnny and Ted started a fire in the old stove while the boys laid out a trail lunch on the table: tea, cocoa, hard tack, canned bully beef, and cheese. Despite the fact that it was cold enough to see one's breath, the air in the cabin quickly warmed up, and the boys and men removed their parkas to relax and shake off the trail's chill.

The cabin was sparsely furnished with two bunk beds, an old plank table with four chairs, roughly constructed cabinets, a wood box, and the wood stove. Their refuge was plain, but after hours on the trail Robin always found it homey and comfortable.

The conversation was light, with many comfortable silences as the four sat sleepily in the now-warm cabin air. With a belly full of food and the morning's trip of cold, fresh air, Robin was tempted to drift off to sleep as he slumped across the table from Wayne.

"Well, boys, we best pack up and get moving. Our light won't last long and an early night's sleep in Tsiigehtchic will do us well for the trail tomorrow."

Johnny's words brought Robin back to life. Stretching lazily, he slowly rose and helped pack up. After the pleasant warmth of the cabin, the afternoon air felt much colder than the temperature of minus twenty-three. Robin shivered, settled into the toboggan, and burrowed under the blankets as the team swung into motion.

The trip now seemed extremely slow. Although Robin had his turns at mushing, he longed to drive the team at full speed, manoeuvring quickly around bends in the trail and cutting past other dog teams in a real race. To finally be out with the dogs but held in check was pure torture.

Once more Robin clambered into the toboggan as Johnny began to break trail and Ted moved back to mush the team. Wayne was mushing the first team now, and Robin watched the back of his head as they gradually moved along. He dragged his mitten-covered hand beside the toboggan and scooped in a handful of snow. Even though it was hard to get the extremely dry snow to ball together, Robin still managed to pack it enough to make a decent-size weapon. What Robin meant to do was hit Wayne in the back. Without so much as a second thought to aim, he wound up and threw, striking Wayne fully in the back of the head. His friend jumped, shrugged, and yelped simultaneously. Wayne's quick reaction surprised the dogs, and they suddenly pulled hard against their traces. As Wayne vainly stretched his right hand forward to grab the handle of the lazy-back, the toboggan lurched forward. In slow motion he flailed backwards and plopped with a thud into the snow.

Ted pulled Dana and the team up behind Wayne as he rolled over in the snow. Despite himself he joined Robin and laughed as Wayne lifted his head and peered out from under his muskrat hat with a look of utter confusion. Ahead of the group, Johnny stopped on his snowshoes and turned back at the commotion. The first thing he spotted was a driverless toboggan heading towards him on the trail. The second thing he saw was Wayne flailing on his belly in the middle of the trail. With a commanding "Whoa," Johnny waved the driverless team down and grabbed the traces. He had no idea what had happened, but the sight of Wayne wallowing in the snow made him chuckle.

Robin climbed out of his toboggan and stood laughing over his friend. Pushing himself to his knees, Wayne glanced up and smiled sheepishly at Robin. By the time Robin noticed that Wayne's smile had transformed from sheepish to wolfish, it was too late. Gathering his weight over his knees, Wayne lunged with full force, tackling Robin square in the waist. With a resounding *ooooffff,* Robin toppled backwards into the snow with Wayne on top. Ted and Johnny moved back as the boys flopped in the snow in a flurry of face washes.

"Okay, okay!" Ted finally shouted. "We're losing daylight fast, so you two yahoos settle down and let's get going. Robin, despite the fact that was a beautiful shot, you can take over for Johnny and break trail for a while."

The boys sat beside each other, trying to catch their breath. At his father's words Robin slumped backwards and lay on the snow. Wayne rubbed him on the head, then helped him to his feet.

Breaking trail was hard work, and Ted didn't intend Robin to stay out front long. He watched his son jog ahead on snowshoes. Although he didn't have to, Wayne had donned his snowshoes, as well, and joined Robin ahead of the dogs. It wasn't long before the boys tired and were relieved of their trail-breaking duties. Back in the toboggan, Robin stretched out and closed his eyes. He couldn't imagine anything more fun than being out with Johnny, Wayne, and his father ...

Robin wasn't sure if he had dozed off, but something was wrong. The toboggan wasn't moving. Sitting up, he looked ahead at the other toboggan. Wayne and Johnny were gone! He glanced back, and Ted was missing, too. Stepping out onto the snow, Robin walked ahead, searching for signs of the others.

"Dad! Johnny! Wayne!" he called out, but silence was his only answer.

At the front of Johnny's team a series of tracks led off into the trees. Robin's heart pounded as he recognized three sets but not a larger fourth one that seemed to follow the others. Despite his fears, Robin broke into a run and followed the tracks into the bush. Branches stung his face as he staggered ahead, staring at the fresh tracks. He fought his way through dense growth and stopped to catch his breath. Bending forward, he placed his hands on his knees and waited for the pain in his oxygen-starved lungs to subside. The tracks continued ahead and over a small hill.

As Robin gathered himself to continue, something snapped in the bushes to his left. He turned, expecting to see his father, but instead caught a glimpse of someone in a dark green parka ducking behind some trees. Robin froze, not knowing whether to cry out or run as fast as he could to get away. Knowing he had been spotted, the person moved from cover and slowly stood erect. Robin saw a rifle in the figure's hands and noticed he was also wearing snowshoes. Panic-stricken, Robin remembered that he hadn't put his snowshoes on before entering the bush. If he had to flee, he wouldn't stand much of a chance.

The figure stared at Robin, his parka hood pulled high, shrouding his face in shadow. Robin couldn't see beyond the shadow but imagined the eyes piercing the darkness and meeting his own. With some inward decision, the figure began to snowshoe towards Robin. Unable to budge, Robin felt as if his legs were detached from his body. By the time he broke out of his trance, his unknown pursuer had already closed the gap between them by half.

Fuelled by outright terror, Robin stumbled ahead. His mukluks sank in the deep snow, and even at a full run he might as well have been wading through water. Robin didn't look back but knew the distance between his stalker and himself was getting shorter. He fell and rose to his feet, only to trip and fall once more. As he threw himself forward and prepared to tumble again, a rough mitten closed over his mouth and jerked him backwards. Robin sniffed gasoline and campfire smoke as he tried to breathe through the scratchy material.

"Don't go near Shildii Rock," a voice rasped. "Don't go near Shildii Rock."

Tearing the mitten from his face, Robin inhaled deeply. He fell forward into the snow and quickly rolled over to face the unknown enemy. Instead he found himself blinking at the starry sky of a late-winter afternoon. He was lying on his back in the toboggan!

Robin sat up, opened his eyes wide, and focused. Ahead, he saw the faint outline of Wayne's back on the other toboggan, with

Johnny jogging in front. Glancing over his shoulder, he glimpsed Ted mushing above him. Exhaling loudly, he slid back into the toboggan. How could dreams seem so real? He could swear that the smell of gasoline and campfire still clung to his face where the mitten had clamped over his mouth and nose. There had to be a way that he could get back to Shildii Rock with Wayne as soon as possible!

Chapter 6

It was a tired crew that arrived in Tsiigehtchic late that evening. Special Constable André Jerome had the police cabin warm and ready. Robin had been convinced he was dying from hunger when they were out on the trail. Now that he sat in the cabin's warmth he wasn't so sure. He picked at the caribou stew that André had prepared, too hungry and too tired to enjoy one of his favourite meals. Wayne had succumbed to exhaustion immediately upon entering the cabin and lay asleep on one of the lower bunks.

Robin excused himself from the table, gingerly stepped on the mattress beside Wayne, and pulled himself into the upper bunk. It felt so good to lie still and relax. He tightened the muscles in his thighs and pointed his toes, quivering as a yawn passed through his body. Rolling onto his side, facing the room, he watched and listened as his father, Johnny, and André talked at the table.

Things had been quiet with not too much to

report in the community. The fishing had been good, and they would take some extra frozen fish back to Fort McPherson in the toboggans. Most people in the community were heading out to winter camps after enjoying time in town between seasons. André had vaccinated most of the dogs in town, but some of the trappers who lived in the bush year-round would need a visit on their next patrol to administer shots.

Robin's eyes grew heavy as the men's voices blended into a relaxing drone. He squinted at the light from the lanterns as it flickered across the ceiling and created a kaleidoscope of shadowy creatures, animals, and adventures. In the morning they would return home. Now that the trail was broken, the trip would be faster and Robin would get to mush. With a smile on his lips, he drifted into a peaceful sleep.

The next day once again brought excellent travelling weather. Ted and Johnny spent the morning with André visiting the community's elders. Robin and Wayne were left to themselves, free to roam and do as they pleased. They wandered along the bank of the river, enjoying the morning and anticipating the day to come.

Spectacularly situated, Tsiigehtchic was on the western bank of the Mackenzie River where it met the Arctic Red River. The burnt red banks of the Mackenzie rose fifty feet above the water, forming cliffs of impressive colour and composition. The Arctic Red River flowed into the Mackenzie on the northern edge of the community. The Mackenzie was roughly a mile wide here, and one could gaze across at the eastern bank, watching hawks and ravens riding the air currents.

The focus of the community was the Roman Catholic church. High atop the bank, its bright whiteness provided a vivid contrast to the red cliffs of the Mackenzie. It seemed to make the whole community glow and stand out from its surroundings. The boys plopped themselves down on the steps of the church and contentedly looked out across the river at the far snow-covered shore.

"I know I keep saying this, Wayne, but I can't get Shildii Rock out of my mind."

"I know what you mean. I've got the matches in my sock drawer and take them out and look at them pretty much every day. Well, to be honest, several times a day."

Robin, who had been staring at the river, turned to Wayne. "Some people have been taking their dogs for runs down the Peel past Shildii already. We can take Dana and the team for a run and get some decent time at Shildii. I know we'll find something."

Wayne nodded. "I bet we find tracks." He paused, then asked, "Are you sure we shouldn't tell our fathers about the whole thing? They might listen, you know."

Robin shrugged. "Sometimes they think we're pretty crazy, and maybe sometimes we are, but this time it's different. I can feel it in my bones. We need to find something first. Something more than a book of matches."

Wayne accepted his friend's words with silence.

"Hey, you two!" Ted Harris waved at the boys from the crest of the hill. "Get the lead out. We have to leave."

"I'm ready to go to Shildii as soon as we can, Robin," Wayne said solemnly as he stood. "We can solve this mystery together."

Robin smiled and put his hand on his friend's shoulder as they sauntered up the hill to where their fathers were preparing for the trip back to Fort McPherson. The toboggans were heavier today with the frozen fish aboard. Even so, the trail that had now been broken would provide a much smoother ride. The boys helped with the loading and hitching of the dogs. They were getting a late start, and the last part of their return would be in complete darkness. A late supper before bed would have to do once they reached their destination.

With a wink, Ted hopped into the carryall. "Lead us out, boys! Johnny and I deserve a rest."

Yawning with exaggeration, Johnny climbed aboard the other toboggan and pretended he was ready to go to sleep. Wayne and Robin exchanged excited grins as they took their positions at the backs of their toboggans.

Ted turned to Robin from his place in the carryall. "Take them out easy, Robin." When he saw the disappointed look on his son's face, he added, "But once they're warmed up, let 'er rip!"

With an excited laugh, Robin nodded. "Okay!" he shouted to Dana. Mouth open in an enthusiastic doggie smile, Dana turned and led the team forward. Each toboggan's load was noticeably several hundred pounds heavier. The dogs would work harder but were anxious for the task at hand. The boys and men waved goodbye to Special Constable Jerome and a few others who had gathered to see them off.

The main team with Dana at lead was much faster than the second team, so with a freshly broken trail, Robin headed out first. He could feel the power of the dogs as they strained to gain speed, and thrilled at the beauty of these well-trained animals. Shouting encouragement, he moved them to full speed. When he glanced back, he saw the distance between his team and Wayne's growing by the second. "Chaw!" he cried as the trail shifted to the right. Robin imagined that Wayne was Danny Francis. "Eat my snow, Danny!" he yelled.

Ted peered up at Robin from the toboggan. "What was that, son?"

Robin blushed. "Nothing, Dad. It's just great to be out here with you and the guys."

Ted nodded. "Slow it down a bit, son. We've got a long day ahead and we don't need the dogs dead tired by mid-afternoon."

Robin braked the team, and the trip settled into a comfortable pace. The four took turns mushing, and the rest of the day passed without event.

The heavier loads on the return trip required extra care with two of the steeper hills. One hill in particular at about halfway required the use of the head rope. The teams stopped at the top of the hill, and the head rope was looped around a tree to take the weight of the first toboggan as it started down the hill. The rope was carefully played out as the team advanced so that the toboggan gradually moved behind the dogs, its weight controlled by letting the rope out bit by bit.

It had been a good two days, and both Robin and Wayne were anxious for more time out with the dogs. They were also ready for more time at Shildii Rock.

Chapter 7

The Hudson's Bay Company store was the centre of activity in Fort McPherson. Along with Krutko's Trading Post, it was one of only two shops in town. Plain in appearance with red shingles, white siding, and red trim, the exterior of the Hudson's Bay store revealed no clue about the bustling activity that took place within. Besides groceries, the store also handled most of the local fur trading and housed the community's post office.

The store was situated at the north end of town on the bank of the Peel River. In summer the men sat out front on benches, chatting as they took in the summer glow of the river and the view of the distant Richardson Mountains. In the winter they gathered inside, using the guise of manly duties and business to conceal the true enjoyment of swapping stories and laughter. If someone wanted the latest gossip or to visit a bit, the Hudson's Bay store provided such diversion along with an hour or so of shopping. That being the case Robin didn't mind when his mother asked him to pick up a few items at the store for her baking.

When Robin entered the store, he paused to savour the sights, sounds, and smells that defined life in a small northern community. The murmur of voices and laughter exchanged between friends who shared experiences and a way of life greeted his ears. The walls were painted plywood and the floor was oiled wood. The strong but not unpleasant odour of moose and caribou hides mingled with the smoky tang of camp and fire; the aroma of furs, duffle cloth, Stroud cloth, and other dry goods; the scent of close-quartered humans; and a whiff of freshly rolled and smoked cigarettes.

Shelves lined the perimeter, and islands had been sporadically spaced to display canned goods and other merchandise throughout the store. Robin moved ahead past the post office counter where Chief John Kay, Robert Alexi, Charlie Snowshoe, and Henri Bertrand chatted and laughed.

Robert Alexi placed a hand on Robin's shoulder, and he turned to face the man. "Now just wait a minute, young fella. Let me take a good look at you. I haven't seen you since early in the summer."

Robin grimaced as the men surveyed him and rumpled his hair.

"Now if I'm not mistaken, this young man's grown a foot since I last saw him," Charlie Snowshoe said.

Robert Alexi grinned. "The last time I saw him, he had to stand on a log to kick a duck in the butt."

The men all guffawed as Robin happily continued to move through the store, which was quite crowded. He recognized many of the elders who were in town: Caroline Kunnizzi, Brian Francis, Lucy Rat, George Vittrekwa, and Old Harriet. Lucy Rat and Old Harriet were very respected in the community. They both had their own trap lines and were amazing women.

With her cotton dress, powder-blue sweater, and red head scarf, Old Harriet looked frumpy and subdued, but her bright, intelligent eyes and the ever-present pipe that hung from the corner of her mouth revealed the strong and lively spirit that burned within. She spoke to Robin in Gwich'in, and he shifted languages without thinking.

"Is your mother at home, Robin?"

"Yes, ma'am."

"Tell her for me that I'll be by to visit for tea and some cookies."

Robin smiled. "I will." Old Harriet loved Robin's mothers' cookies, and she always took a kerchief full when she finished her visits at the Harris home.

"Mussi cho," she said, thanking Robin.

Robin's mother had asked him to pick up some Carnation canned milk. Where on earth he would find it he had no idea. He knelt in front of a shelf and half-heartedly shifted through an assortment of beans and soups. Why did his mother need canned milk, anyway? Her baking was great, but why couldn't she just use powdered milk as they did for everything else?

Standing, Robin moved to the next row, stepped back to survey the shelves, and felt something brush his arm. He turned and ploughed chest first into a flat cart stacked high with boxes and other food containers. A box near the top teetered, then fell with a resounding crash to the floor. Cans of peas splayed out of the top and rolled in all directions across the floor. Robin stood frozen in place, not knowing which can to chase down first.

"Aw, for Pete's sake!" a voice cried from behind the remaining boxes. An angry face peered around the stacks. When the face saw who had knocked the box over, its angry expression was replaced with surprise, then clouded with anger again, eyes squinting.

"I'm sorry, Timothy! I was trying to find some evaporated milk for my mom and didn't even hear you come up behind me."

Timothy planted his hands on his hips aggressively. "So it's my fault then?"

Robin sighed. "That's not what I said."

"Timothy, what's going on here?" A tall man with whitish-blond hair approached the boys from the front of the store. "Did you do this, young man?" he demanded as his gaze settled on Robin.

"No, Dad, it's my fault. I tried to turn the corner too quickly and I guess I piled the boxes too high."

Robin arched an eyebrow at the unexpected statement from Timothy.

"Well, I'm sorry I was about to blame you, young man, for Timothy's mistake. I'm Henry Parch, Timothy's father."

"I'm Robin Harris ... a friend of Timothy's from school."

It was Timothy's turn to raise an eyebrow in surprise.

"Well, boys, I'll leave the two of you to clean this up while I get back to work." Henry Parch headed back towards the front of the store. "It was nice to meet you, Robin!" he shouted over his shoulder.

The boys knelt together and started to gather the cans of peas. They worked in silence, neither one knowing exactly what to say. "You ... why?" both boys began at the same time.

"Go ahead, Robin," Timothy said, looking down at the cans.

"Why did you cover for me? I was going to

tell your dad that it was my fault, anyway. You didn't have to do it."

"I know I didn't but, well, you covered for me in science class, and I guess I've been pretty much a creep to you guys."

Robin nodded. "You sure have."

"You didn't have to agree so fast," Timothy said quietly, glancing down once more. "Why ... why did you say I was your friend?"

"I thought you could use one. Even though you've been pretty much a creep, I had this feeling you weren't that bad a guy. I'd still like to stick your head in that big volcano you made in science class, though!"

Timothy stopped lifting cans back into place and stared at the one in his hand. "I guess I've just been mad about a lot of things. My mom and dad were divorced last year. Mom moved away and then Dad decided to move here. First my mom's gone and then all of my friends are gone, too. I hate this place for being so far away from my mom. I hate my dad for bringing me here." Timothy had started to speak louder, but now he lowered his voice once more. "And I guess I kind of hated you, Wayne, and everyone else for just being here."

Robin scratched his head. "That doesn't seem fair. We didn't have anything to do with your coming here or what happened between your mom and dad. We're actually pretty nice guys once you get to know us."

Timothy sighed. "I'm sure you are."

The boys picked up the last of the cans and stood beside the cart. Timothy reached over to a shelf on the far side of the cart, handed Robin a can of Carnation milk, and shrugged. "I help my dad stock the shelves, so I pretty much know where everything is."

Robin grabbed the can. "Thanks. I'm kind of late, so I better get moving."

Timothy nodded and began to push the cart past Robin.

"Hey, Timothy!" Robin shouted.

Timothy turned.

Smiling, Robin said, "See you at school."

Timothy's face split into just about the biggest grin Robin had ever seen. Then he gave a quick wave and moved off into the store.

Chapter 8

It almost felt as if school had started all over again, but in a good way this time. Robin, Wayne, and Timothy found something new to do or talk about each and every day. Even old Mr. Debark seemed easier to get along with.

The first day of school after Robin and Timothy had their encounter at the Hudson's Bay store, Robin invited Timothy to play catch with Wayne and Billy. He was quiet at first, but it didn't take long for the boys to start playing freely and the past was soon forgotten. The boys were amazed at how much fun Timothy really was, and he in turn couldn't believe he had been so rotten to them in the first place.

Timothy told the boys stories about life in Winnipeg — the buildings, restaurants, movies to see and the hockey games to play and watch. For their part Robin and Wayne tried to teach Timothy what life in a northern town was all about. Even though it had been months since Timothy had moved there, he really didn't know anything about the place and hadn't done anything other than go to school and work at the store. The weird thing was it seemed as if Timothy actually began to have fun and was becoming interested in what there was to do around Fort McPherson.

Wayne's grandfather made Timothy a pair of snowshoes and helped the boys set rabbit snares on some of the small trails in the bush near town. Timothy convinced his father to let him practise target shooting with the boys, and he learned how to handle a .22 rifle. Wayne was a fantastic marksman and was patient as Timothy got the hang of things. Timothy was quite athletic, and the boys soon learned there was no way they could catch him on foot or on snowshoes. He was a natural, and the boys plotted how their new friend would win the snowshoe race in the New Year's Festival.

Henry Parch was happy that his son seemed to be finally fitting in. He agreed to give Timothy more time off in the afternoons when school was over so the boy could visit with his new buddies. Most of the time the kids headed to the RCMP compound and fed the dogs, or hung out at Robin's or Wayne's houses just talking and laughing about the events of the day. It was a situation none of the boys would have guessed possible a few weeks earlier.

"Wayne, what are you up to this weekend?" Robin asked one Friday evening in Wayne's bedroom.

"I don't think we're doing much of anything," Wayne said. "Why?"

"I was just wondering. Dad said I could take the dogs out on Sunday if the weather was okay."

Wayne grinned at Robin, then glanced at Timothy.

"Sounds like fun," Timothy said gloomily. "Whatever you guys are up to I can't come. Dad said I have to help move stock on Sunday at the store."

Robin looked at Wayne questioningly, and Wayne shrugged.

"Timothy, if Wayne and I helped you move stock on Saturday, do you think your dad would let you come with us to Shildii Rock by dog team on Sunday?"

"Yeah, sure! As long as the work gets done, I think my dad would let me do anything."

"Now here's the best part," Robin whispered as he closed Wayne's bedroom door. He explained in detail what he had seen at Shildii Rock, and Wayne showed Timothy the precious book of matches.

Timothy listened to everything, nodding thoughtfully from time to time. "Wow, it does seem like something's going on. What's so special about Shildii Rock, anyway?"

"There's a legend that's been passed down by the Gwich'in people for years," Wayne said. "There once was an old man who lived with his wife, three sons, and a daughter. The daughter, Ts'eh'in, was said to possess magical powers. In summer they fished and camped at Scraper Hill, what we call Deeddhoo Goonli. One day the old man spoke to his boys. He said, 'My children, I am hungry for meat. I want food. Go to the mountains.' The sons left and the daughter remained behind with the old man and her mother. The boys travelled to the Richardson Mountains west of Fort McPherson. They were gone for a long time.

"The mother knew about her daughter's powers and spoke to her. 'My daughter, soon your brothers will be returning. When they do, you must not look at them and you must not say anything.' At that time around Shildii Rock there was nothing but barren land. There were no willows on the hill. From where the girl stood, if she looked downriver, it would be easy to see her brothers returning. Her mother knew this.

"Soon she became very lonesome for her brothers and was anxious for them to come back. Though her mother warned her, she forgot what she was told. One day she saw her brothers walking towards her.

"'Mother, my brothers are coming home!' she cried. All at once the three brothers were turned to stone — three rock pillars in a row. The dog that was with them also turned to stone. That's what Shildii Rock is." Wayne paused before continuing. "Their mother was cooking bannock when this happened, and they say that it, too, was turned to stone. Today, if you look carefully at Scraper Hill, you'll see the stones used to bake her bannock."

"That's pretty neat," Timothy said. "I wonder if any of the legends up here are true."

"My dad sure believes in them," Wayne said. "He says that every time someone disrespects the beliefs of the Gwich'in, something will happen that proves the legends are true."

"Legends aren't the only neat things about Fort McPherson and the North," Robin added. "A lot of interesting stuff's happened here over the years. Have you ever heard about the Mad Trapper of Rat River?"

Timothy nodded. "You bet I have! We learned about him in school."

"He had his camp up near Rat River. In the end he was shot on the Eagle River in the Yukon. If you remember, he was a pretty crafty guy. He wounded one RCMP member and killed another. Then he led a posse of police and trappers on a pretty good chase. In the end they tracked him down and didn't have any choice but to shoot him. They never did figure out who he was. My dad built a cairn on the spot where the Mountie was shot and killed."

"That's neat," Timothy said. "Hey, is old Lucy Rat named after the Rat River?"

"No, actually, the river's named after Lucy Rat's husband, Charlie Rat, because he had his camp at the mouth of the Rat River."

"She's a great old lady," Timothy said, and the other boys nodded.

Robin smiled and folded his arms across his chest. "Another thing people don't know about the North is that this is where hockey was invented."

Timothy smirked. "It was not!"

Wayne nodded. "It really was, Timothy. Deline's a community south of here in the Mackenzie Valley. Sir John Franklin, the famous explorer, was there years ago, and they found the remains of Old Fort Franklin that were left behind. Some of the papers they found that dated back to 1825 talked about them playing a game called hockey on skates. That makes it the first recorded history of hockey being played anywhere!"

"Wow, I didn't know half this stuff!" Timothy said, shaking his head.

"Forget about all that," Robin said. "What I really want to know right now is what's going on at Shildii Rock."

The boys sat in silence on Wayne's bed. Even though no words were spoken, they all knew Sunday couldn't come soon enough.

Chapter 9

Saturday was a long day of hard work. Henry Parch agreed to let Timothy have Sunday off if the boys helped out and all of the shelves were completely restocked. The three boys started at 8:30 in the morning and finally finished at 5:30 that afternoon. They were tired but excited about the next day.

On Sunday morning Timothy watched as Wayne and Robin put the dogs in place and hitched the team. Ted supervised but really didn't have to do much. Both Wayne and Robin had been watching their fathers do this from a young age and helped out whenever possible. By any standards they were experienced dog handlers.

"So where are you boys headed?" Ted asked. He noted a quick look exchanged between Wayne and Robin but didn't give it much thought. The two were always concocting some adventure together. They were good boys, and as long as they stayed out of trouble, Ted wasn't concerned.

"I figured we'd run the dogs on the Peel a bit, Dad. Wayne and Tim will add a bit of weight. After that we'll do a few trails and stuff. I just want some practice. Tim's pretty anxious to go for a dog team ride and see some of the trails, too."

Ted gazed thoughtfully at the three boys, then smiled. "That sounds good, son. But don't run them too hard and make sure you get back before dark. You only have a couple of hours right now, so you better get going." Ted put his hand on Robin's shoulder as Wayne and Timothy clambered into the carryall. "Billy doesn't stand a chance this year, son."

Robin grinned, stepped onto the back of the toboggan, and cried, "Okay!"

The dogs were off in a shot. Ted watched as the boys receded into the distance. He smiled as he caught snatches of their chatter and laughter. Then they were gone. Ted turned and headed towards the single men's quarters. A new constable, Grant Abernathy, was coming in, and Ted wanted everything to be ready for his arrival. With Grant and Johnny they would be at full staff for the detachment.

Robin urged the dogs into a full run. He loved the feel of their power as they surged ahead. With Christmas and the New Year's race just weeks away he needed to get more training in with the dogs. Timothy turned and waved at Robin, then said something to Wayne, causing them both to laugh. Robin was glad that Timothy was enjoying himself. He had proved to be a great friend, and Robin wanted him to enjoy his new home at Fort McPherson.

"Chaw!" Robin shouted, imagining how he would move the dogs around turns on the river. On the way back from Shildii they would find a trail or two to do some tight turns and hills.

As they approached Shildii Rock, Robin was seized with dread. He could see the rock looming ahead on the riverbank and glanced at his friends, who smiled and laughed ahead of him in the toboggan. For a moment, to Robin, the rock cast a shadow that blotted out those smiles. It was all he could do not to turn the dogs around and head back to town as fast as they would run. But as much as he was afraid, he knew he had to see what lay ahead.

The dogs rapidly covered the remaining distance to shore. "Whoa!" Robin commanded, halting the dogs and securing the team. Wayne and Timothy got out of the toboggan and stood beside Robin, gazing up at Shildii Rock.

"Now what?" Timothy asked.

Wayne studied the area where they had stopped. "Well, guys, I don't see any tracks. It hasn't snowed recently or been very windy, so if anyone's been here in the past few days, they would have left tracks. I don't see any tracks leading up to the rock, either." Wayne indicated where the trail led up to the rock through the willows. He was right. There were no tracks, just light, fluffy snow.

Both Wayne and Timothy looked at Robin, expecting confirmation or comment. But all he did was stare up at Shildii Rock.

Timothy opened his mouth to speak, but Wayne touched him on the arm and whispered, "He gets like this sometimes. I think he's just disappointed."

After another moment, Robin finally said, "I'm not disappointed." He walked towards the toboggan and dug inside the carryall. "There are tracks up top and plenty more. I can feel it."

Timothy and Wayne exchanged uneasy glances. They watched as Robin dug out his snowshoes and secured them to his mukluks.

"What are you guys waiting for?" Robin asked.

"But, Robin, there aren't any tracks," Timothy said, not too sure of himself.

"That doesn't mean there can't be tracks coming in from another direction. If you wanted to hide the fact you were here, would you leave tracks all over the shore in plain view of the main trail on the river?"

Timothy opened his mouth to speak, but this time he glanced at Wayne first. Closing his eyes in defeat, Wayne slowly shook his head and walked over to the toboggan to retrieve his snowshoes. Timothy looked up at the rock and back at his new friends. What was he getting into?

The boys climbed the bank in silence, passing through the willows and winding up the steady incline, each with their own thoughts of what might be ahead. Robin had overcome his initial feelings of trepidation and now excitedly led the group forward. He wasn't put off by the fact that they hadn't seen any tracks. Robin knew he had a vivid imagination. However, he also knew that when he felt this strongly about something he was usually right.

Wayne, for his part, was happy to be out with friends and the dogs. Without any tracks or other signs, he was sure Robin was leading them on another wild-goose chase, something he was used to.

Everything was new and thrilling for Timothy. A few days ago he had hated this place, but now it was full of adventure. The dog team was incredible! He thought Robin was a little nuts, but looking for spies or whatever they were doing was fun, too.

When the boys reached the top, they first checked the area where Wayne and Robin had seen the trail in the bush before the snow came. There were no tracks to be found. They spread out and fanned across the top of the bank, searching for signs of life. Other than animal tracks they didn't see a thing. Wayne and Timothy stood by Shildii Rock and watched as Robin explored the area where the snow had now been packed by their snowshoes.

"When's he going to stop?" Timothy asked.

Wayne smiled. "Knowing Robin, it might be a while. He's a pretty determined guy. One spring when we were camping near Tsiigehtchic he wandered into the woods to go to the bathroom. He came running back to camp, telling everyone he'd seen a polar bear. Well, everyone knows polar bears don't come down this far, but he insisted he'd seen one. Our dads actually humoured him by looking around a bit, but we all finally went to bed. All of us except Robin. It was pretty light out already that time of year, and he sat up all night going down to the river and stuff." Wayne stopped and glanced at Robin.

"Did he finally give up?" Timothy asked.

"Actually, at about four in the morning we all woke up because there was this hooting and hollering by the river. We hurried down there, and there was Robin running along the shore knee-deep in the water, hollering and pointing upriver. Sure enough there was a polar bear wading into the water and swimming across to the other side."

"You're kidding?"

"No, I'm not. It was a real live polar bear. It was pretty scrawny and scraggly. Everyone figured it was old or sick and couldn't get food, so it wandered all the way down from Tuktoyaktuk or something. It was pretty amazing. If Robin hadn't stayed up all night, we might have never seen it."

The boys watched as Robin moved farther away and into the bushes. "Let's go, Tim. He's headed in the direction of the trail we saw going into the bush."

Wayne and Timothy entered the bush where Robin had disappeared and followed his tracks. They could see ahead now. Robin had stopped in a small clearing. He held his head cocked to one side as if listening to something. Timothy and Wayne halted beside him and listened intently.

Wayne sniffed the air and nodded. "I smell it, too, Robin."

Timothy looked puzzled and sniffed in every direction as hard as he could. Then he smelled it, too. "Smoke?"

"Smoke," Wayne confirmed.

"Robin, did you smell it all the way back at the rock?" Timothy asked, trying not to sound too amazed.

"It's from all the time he's spent with great Gwich'in hunters like me," Wayne said on Robin's behalf. "Once you've learned the ways of the land, you start to see, smell, and hear things before they're even there."

Robin had a quirky smile on his face, which now turned a bright shade of red. "Actually, Wayne, until you mentioned it, I didn't smell a thing. I was embarrassed about us not finding anything, so I came in here to be alone."

Timothy snickered, and everyone laughed.

"So, it was I, the great Gwich'in hunter, who first smelled the smoke," Wayne said.

Robin rolled his eyes. "Geez."

"Look," Timothy said, pointing at the sky above the evergreens. At first glance nothing was visible. After a moment of intense inspection, the faintest wisps of smoke could be seen against the clouds and blue sky.

"That's not very far off inland," Robin said. "We've got enough daylight left. Let's go for it." He looked at the other boys. "Are you with me?"

"You betcha!" Timothy replied.

Wayne nodded silently, and all three moved in the direction of the smoke.

Even with snowshoes the going wasn't easy. The trees were thicker farther away from the river. Without knowing exactly how close to the source of the smoke they were, the boys had to push quietly through the branches and small bushes to limit the noise as much as possible. That meant moving even slower. Wayne was light on his feet and always picked the best trails. He led them expertly.

Robin felt butterflies in his stomach as they crept forward. They were close to finding out something big; he could feel it in his bones. The trees were taller, and now that they were deep in the bush they couldn't look up to see how close they were to the smoke. The smell didn't seem to be getting any stronger, either.

Suddenly, Wayne held his hand up and crouched low to the snow. The boys quickly ducked and crept up to where Wayne had positioned himself. Wayne leaned back without turning his head. "There's a trail straight ahead," he whispered.

Sure enough they could see that a trail had been beaten into the snow. It moved east to west, parallel to the Peel River in the distance.

"If we follow it east, I bet you it curls back to the river," Robin said excitedly.

"Which means if we follow it west it likely leads to where the smoke's coming from," Timothy added.

"That's right, Tim. What are we waiting for?" Robin motioned for Timothy and Wayne to follow him.

Instead of walking on the trail, Robin led the boys through the bush beside it to stay out of sight. Progress was slower, but they were safer and there was less chance of being spotted.

"Oh, boy, here we go," Wayne said to Timothy. "I don't like this, but we better follow him."

The boys caught up to Robin as he moved alongside the trail. They could tell that the trail was well travelled, since the snow was hard-packed. The trail was also narrow enough so that it was hard to spot unless someone stumbled right onto it. To the boys it seemed as if they had been following the trail for a long time, and they wondered if they would ever find anything. It was tiring moving through the brush on snow-shoes, and Robin couldn't tell if he was out of breath from the exertion or the anticipation of what they might find.

Quietly, Wayne reached over and grabbed Robin by the shoulder, stopping him in his tracks and making him sit backwards in the snow. With eyes wide he frantically pointed ahead over Robin's shoulder. Robin hadn't seen a thing. He squinted intently, and the details Wayne had already detected slowly came into focus.

The trail wound ahead and came to a dead end at a large rock formation. A thin wisp of smoke rose lazily into the sky from somewhere in that formation. On closer inspection the boys saw that branches had been used to build up a structure at the front of the rocks and a canvas was being used for additional protection under the branches.

"A perfect spot for a camp," Wayne said.

"Crafty and smart," Robin added.

"Whoever built it doesn't want to be seen," Wayne said. "The rock and branches look so natural. If you weren't looking for it, you wouldn't see it. The way they have the canvas and the branches gives them protection, and it also makes the smoke spread out so it's hard to see."

Timothy moved forward from where he was crouching beside Wayne. "The trail seems to go behind the rocks to the left. Do you think we should take a look?"

Wayne shook his head. "We don't know if anyone's in the shelter or behind the rocks or somewhere else. We should just sit here for a bit and see what happens."

Robin shifted on his heels and surveyed everything in sight. Wayne and Timothy watched him and held their breath, wondering what their friend was going to do next. Finally, Robin lurched ahead in a low crouch to the left of the camp.

"Why me?" Wayne sighed, glancing skyward. "This can't be good."

"Let's just stay here," Timothy pleaded.

"I'm with you, Tim, but as much as it scares me, Robin might need us. Let's keep going behind him."

Robin slunk through the bush, captivated by the thought of what lay on the other side of the rocks. He moved out of sight, and Timothy and Wayne scrambled to catch up. When they manoeuvred around the rocks and spotted Robin, he was frantically waving for them to join him. As they rushed ahead on all fours, they both spotted the cause of Robin's excitement at the same time.

"Unbelievable!" Wayne whispered.

"Unbelievable!" Timothy echoed.

"Robin," Wayne said, "my people have been in this area for years and I haven't heard anyone talk about a cave. How couldn't it be noticed?"

"I don't know, Wayne. Maybe there were trees over the entrance or something. Maybe it wasn't meant to be found." Robin stared at the cave. "This is too good to be true. A secret camp, a secret cave. Now all we need is to find the bad guys."

"I can live without that part," Timothy moaned.

As soon as Timothy finished speaking, a parka hood stuck out of the cave followed by the rest of an entire body. The hood cast a shadow that hid the face from view. The person turned and pulled a bucket from inside the cave, then stood to full height and glanced suspiciously in all directions before seemingly glaring at the three boys where they cowered in the bushes.

Suddenly, Robin sucked in his breath and, with a gasp, fell back. Wayne had no chance to react to his friend's movement and flailed backwards into Timothy. With the full weight of both Robin and Wayne pressing against him, Timothy crumpled. The crackle of breaking branches and twigs rang loud in Timothy's ears as his two friends crushed him. The weight became heavier as Wayne pushed Robin away and tried to pull himself off Timothy.

"Run!" Robin shouted.

Timothy managed to roll onto his stomach and struggle to his snowshoe-clad feet. He spied Wayne and Robin snowshoeing as quickly as possible through the bush. Without looking back he rushed after them as fast as his snowshoes would carry him.

"Hey!" a voice behind him yelled. "You there! Stop or I'll shoot!"

Timothy clambered over the snow, panic gripping his heart and making his lungs feel tight in his chest. He didn't hear any shots but didn't dare slow down. When he caught up to the other boys, he cut past them through the bushes. He could see the brush thin out ahead and he burst out onto the bank behind Shildii Rock. Without missing a step he ran across the clearing above the river and jumped over the edge of the bank. He sailed a good twenty feet through the air before he landed in stride and kept sliding and snowshoeing down the bank. His descent was quick, and he soon stood panting beside the dogs that were now noisily barking and tugging at their traces. If not for Dana's calm, they would have taken off at full speed.

As Wayne and Robin crashed down the bank, Wayne screamed at Timothy, "Get your snowshoes off!"

All three of them ripped their snowshoes off and hurled them into the toboggan.

"Okay!" Robin bellowed as he dived for the

handles of the lazy-back.

Wayne and Timothy both leaped for the now-moving toboggan, toppling inside in a tangled heap of arms and legs.

"Move! Okay! Go! Go! Go!" Robin shouted.

The dogs were in full motion, and Dana seemed to sense the urgency of the moment. She threw every fibre into the traces, and the dogs glided across the snow at an incredible speed. Robin's mind began to clear of panic as he looked back over his shoulder. An icy chill passed through him. There was no mistaking what he saw. The faceless, hooded figure stood motionless beside Shildii Rock, rifle half raised to one shoulder. Robin couldn't see through the shadows, but he knew a pair of eyes glowered at the boys as they fled.

Chapter 10

"You can't be serious!" Wayne jumped up from his bed where he had been sitting and paced to the other side of the room. Robin and Timothy remained sitting on the edge of the bed as Wayne turned and placed his hands on his hips. "We've got to tell our fathers about this. That guy threatened to shoot Tim. He chased us! He's hiding up there and doesn't want to be found for some reason. Don't you think your dad would want to know about that?"

"You know what my father will say," Robin said. "I can just hear him. After he gives me that 'Here we go again' look, he'll tell me how we snuck into someone's camp, surprised the guy, and started to run away from him instead of staying to say hello. Lots of people wouldn't like that and would feel threatened. So the guy grabs his rifle and shouts, 'Stop or I'll shoot!' But he doesn't shoot, does he? He just says that to scare us off because he's a law-abiding citizen who was surprised by some sneaky kids. He just wanted to be left alone."

"Come on, Robin!" Wayne said, exasperated. "He's hiding up there and you know it!"

"I know it and you and Timothy know it, but to my dad it won't seem like that."

Timothy cleared his throat. "Robin's right, Wayne. You know how adults are. Instead of being interested or on our side, they'll give us heck for sneaking up on somebody and scaring him. I think we need to go back and see exactly what's in that cave."

"What?" Robin and Wayne gasped at the same time.

"Well, not right away!" Timothy shot back defensively. "We give that guy time to calm down. In a week or so we go back and see what's in the cave. Then, when we have proof of something once and for all, we go to Robin's dad."

Wayne walked over and flopped down between his two friends. They remained silent for a while, each with his own thoughts, trying to figure out what to do next.

Then Robin spoke. "Tim's right, Wayne. I know that guy's up to no good, but what's my father going to do? Even if he agrees to take a look, so what? He marches into this guy's camp and says hi to him. They have a nice cup of tea, he's real polite and nice to my dad, and that's the end of it. Without some proof of something my dad can't search his stuff."

Wayne scowled. "I don't like it. I know we're going to get into trouble for this somehow. Why don't you at least try to tell your dad about it? If he won't listen, he won't listen. But at least we tried."

Robin shrugged. "Okay, Wayne, I'll talk to my dad. You guys wait here until I get back."

It was a short walk from Wayne's house to the RCMP office, and Robin didn't have much time to decide what he was going to say. When he stepped out of the cold into the small, warm building, he heard two voices in the inner part of the office. Robin poked his head around the corner and saw his father and another RCMP officer.

"Hey, Robin, come over here and meet Constable Abernathy! Grant, this is my son, Robin."

"How are you, Robin?" Grant Abernathy said, extending his hand.

Robin shook the constable's hand and smiled. "Pleased to meet you, sir."

"Just call me Grant. Your dad's getting me organized here so I can settle in and help him out with things."

"Robin, Grant and I are heading over to the Hudson's Bay store so I can introduce him to everyone there. Johnny's joining us and then we're going over to Chief Kay's place. If you want to tag along, you're more than welcome." Ted turned away and said, "Grant, the people here are great and you can expect a warm reception. You came at a great time of year. Everyone's coming in for Christmas and you'll get to meet pretty much all of the community over the next few weeks."

Robin stood back and listened to the men talk. When his father stopped for a breath, he seized his chance. "Dad, I need to tell you about something we saw. I think we —"

"Robin, that's great, but not now. Grant, I better show you where we keep the rabies vaccine and other medicines."

"Dad, there's this weird guy at Shildii Rock. You have to —"

"Robin, I don't have time for your games, okay?" Giving Robin a pat on the head, Ted turned back to the new constable. "Grant, let's take a quick look at the feed shack and the ice house. You'll catch on to how we organize things here pretty quick."

The men walked off, leaving Robin alone in the office. Shaking his head, he silently slipped out the door and returned to Wayne's house. Timothy and Wayne heard Robin come into the house and anxiously stared at him as he entered Wayne's bedroom. He didn't speak and dejectedly slumped onto the floor beside Wayne's bed.

"Well?" Wayne asked finally.

"I tried to tell him, guys, but he wouldn't listen. I hate to say I told you so, but, hey, I did."

"Wayne," Timothy added gravely, "we have to keep quiet about this, and when we get a chance, we have to see what's inside that cave."

All Wayne could do was shake his head in defeat. "Now instead of one crazy friend I have two crazy friends! What did I do wrong in life to deserve this? It's not bad enough that they're both crazy, they both want to go back to Shildii Rock and look in a cave where a lunatic lives with his rifle. Why not? If they want to get shot, I should want to get shot, too!"

Robin and Timothy gave Wayne a hard shove.

"Listen, guys," Robin said, turning serious, "if we can solve the mystery at Shildii Rock, we'll be heroes. We might even get medals or something."

Wayne and Timothy grabbed pillows and began to pummel Robin over the head as he protested in vain.

Chapter 11

Christmas in Fort McPherson was Robin's favourite time of the year. Thoughts of Shildii Rock were once again put aside as the excitement of the season gripped the small town. The cave and the shadowy figure were never far from Robin's mind, but Christmas and all of its trappings made them seem less important for the time being.

The night of the Christmas feast was the best part of all. It was the Friday before Christmas, and everyone was in town. The ladies had spent the better part of a day preparing food and getting the community hall ready. Everything was next to perfect!

As usual Robin drove Ted and Marjorie crazy until they agreed to head over to the hall. And as usual they were among the first ones there. Ted and Marjorie really didn't mind, and it was actually fun to watch everyone arrive.

Johnny and Rachel Reindeer with Wayne and his sister arrived early. John Kay, Charlie

Snowshoe, Robert Alexi, Henri Bertrand, and the new constable, Grant Abernathy, came soon after. Many of the elders arrived together — Brian Francis, Lucy Rat, Old Harriet, Caroline Kunizzi, and others. It didn't take long before the little hall was crowded and noisy with the chatter of adults and the loudness created by the children as they scampered about.

Robin and Wayne waved when Timothy arrived with his father. They had been a little worried that Timothy and Mr. Parch might not show up. Mr. Parch hadn't gone out much since arriving in town, so this was his first true taste of northern hospitality and fun. Everyone went out of their way to make him and Grant Abernathy feel at home. Robin could see both men relax as the community and spirit of the season took over.

The evening started with an incredible feast of wild meat, bannock, fish, soup, and other dishes the women had prepared. Everyone, including Wayne and Robin, watched the new folks in town. They knew an evening like this one usually meant favourite pranks would be played on the newcomers. Robin and Wayne sat back and observed Grant Abernathy, Timothy, and Mr. Parch as they were served steaming bowls of soup.

Timothy took a sip and smiled at his friends, giving them a thumb's up. The boys smiled back, repeating the gesture and stifling giggles as much as possible. Almost on cue Timothy and Grant Abernathy stopped eating and took long looks at their soup. The room exploded with laughter as both victims lifted their spoons for closer inspection. Their mouths dropped open as the eyeball of a caribou stared back at them from their spoons! Robin and Wayne howled at the surprise on Timothy's face as he realized his soup was peering back at him. Even Mr. Debark, who had arrived late, grinned, which Robin found hard to believe. Timothy shook his fist at Robin and Wayne.

Timothy's father, who had also discovered an eyeball, opened his mouth wide and spooned it in. He began to chew, coughed, and chewed some more. Everyone, including the boys, gawked in disbelief. Starting to laugh, Mr. Parch opened his now-empty mouth, then held up the eyeball in his hand. Somehow he had snuck it out of his mouth when he coughed! Everyone laughed all the harder when they realized their own trick had been turned around on them.

Once the meal was over the tables were cleared away and the dancing began. With music provided by guitar and fiddle, the dance would last into the early hours of the morning. The double jig, reel of eight, brandy, and rabbit dance were just some of the favourites. Robin, Wayne, and Timothy sat back and enjoyed one another's company as the adults danced, laughed, and visited with friends and relatives.

Timothy grinned. "This is great! Christmas back home —" He stopped and glanced at the boys. "Christmas in Winnipeg was nothing like this. I can't remember having this much fun ever!"

"It's great, isn't it?" Robin said dreamily as he stared out at the dancers. Although he had been anxious for the night to begin, he was tired and could hardly keep his eyes open. He had a bit of a headache and wondered if he was catching a cold. That was great! All he needed was to be sick for Christmas. "You know, guys, as much fun as this is, I'm feeling tired and a bit sick. I think I'm going to head home."

"Aw, come on, you wimp!" Wayne said.

Timothy studied Robin carefully. "Actually, Wayne, he does look kind of pale."

Wayne peered at his friend and nodded. "He's right, Robin. You are looking a little pasty."

"You guys have fun. If I get some sleep, I'm sure I'll feel better in the morning." The boys stood up with Robin as he got ready to leave.

"If you feel better tomorrow, Robin, drop by the store," Timothy said.

"I will, Tim. You guys have fun," Robin said as he walked over to his parents to tell them he was leaving.

Marjorie Harris felt her son's head. "You are

a bit hot, but it's very hot in here, too." She looked at Ted.

"Marj, if the boy wants to go home in the middle of the Christmas feast, then I think he must be sick."

Robin tried to smile at his father but couldn't muster much more than a grimace.

"Okay, Robin," his mother said, "you bundle up and I'll come home with you. Maybe a bit of lemon tea will make you feel better."

"Aw, Mom, I don't want to spoil your night. You stay here with Dad. I'll be fine. I promise to go right to bed. Maybe I'll make some tea first."

"He's right, Marj. You stay here. We won't be long, son. Be sure to do the zipper on your parka to the top and keep your hood up all the way home. After I drag your mom onto the dance floor a few more times, we'll be along shortly."

"Okay, Dad."

Marjorie watched her son wander into the coatroom and emerge a moment later with his parka on. With a halfhearted wave he pulled up his hood and headed into the night.

"Don't worry, Marj," Ted said, putting his arm around his wife. "Our big boy will be fine. Now where's that dance we were talking about?" With that Ted took his wife by the hand and danced her onto the floor in a fast jig.

Home was close by, and in a town like Fort McPherson, night was nothing to be afraid of.

It was dark almost all day long at this time of year, anyway, so nobody really took notice. No one locked their doors and no one had anything to fear. Robin trudged through the cold night air with no sound but the *hush, hush, hush* of his mukluks on the snow to keep him company. He gazed at the sky where the northern lights were putting on their own celebration of the season. The milky greens and soft pale blues swirled across the sky in ever-shifting patterns.

Robin took a deep breath and watched as the warm air exhaled from his lungs left a steamy path. As he navigated along the main trail, he caught the sweet smell of cigarette smoke. The sounds of voices carried through the night, and Robin stopped to listen. The only buildings in the vicinity were storage sheds, and he couldn't figure out why anyone would stop there for a conversation. Listening carefully, he followed the sounds and found himself against the side of one of the larger sheds. He heard the voices clearly now coming from the far side. His heart ran cold as he moved closer to the corner where the voices became louder. There was no mistaking the loudest one. It belonged to Fritz!

Ever since the night Fritz had fought his father he had stayed clear whenever he saw the Dutchman. Still, he would never forget that voice, and now its very sound froze Robin where he stood. He didn't recognize the other voice, but it had a peculiar accent. Robin had never heard anything like it before. One thing he did recognize, however, which was very unusual, was the fear registering in Fritz's voice. Robin pressed against the shed and moved within inches of the corner. The men were now standing only a few feet from him.

"You haven't done a very good job, Fritz. I don't think I picked a good partner."

"No, you wrong," Fritz said hurriedly, a slight tremble in his voice. "Fritz good partner. He make sure no one find out."

"It's too late for that already. Those kids are snooping around and were right at the cave the other day. It's up to you, Fritz, to get their attention somewhere else. Change the scent, so to speak. In Montana we'd call it laying the bluff thick."

Montana! Robin's heart skipped a beat. That accent! It was American! He moved even closer to the corner of the shed. Despite the fear that threatened to snatch the very breath from deep in his lungs, he needed to get a look at the stranger with Fritz. The voices became very low, and he had to strain to listen.

"Fritz, I don't tolerate people who mess up a job. If you don't take care of those boys soon, I'm going to take care of you."

"Don't vorry! Fritz vill —"

"I don't worry. I take care of my business, Fritz.

You just make sure you take care of yours!"

"I vill, I vill. Everyting vill be okie-dokie. Fritz promise!"

Everything became quiet and then Robin heard footsteps retreating in the other direction. Robin shivered in the shadows. His breathing slowly returned to normal and he felt his body relax. Slowly, he stepped around the corner and squinted into the darkness where the men had walked away just moments before. If only he could have stolen just one glance. Robin scuffed the toe of his mukluk on the snow and glanced at the ground.

"Vell, if it ain't da smartie pants police boy himself."

Robin jumped in his parka and recoiled as Fritz stepped from the shadows.

"So you vere listening to old Fritz and his friend, vere you?"

"Well, I, no, I was just walking home and I decided to come this way."

"You think Fritz stupid?"

"No, Mr. Fritz, but I have to get home. My mom … my dad will miss me."

Robin backed away, but Fritz quickly leaned forward and grabbed him by the arm. "So you stick your long nose where it don't belong. Looking for trouble, no?"

Robin couldn't speak but shook his head quickly from side to side. Fritz moved closer and pushed his face next to Robin's ear. Robin closed his eyes. Fritz's breath reeked of homebrew. Robin felt sick to his stomach.

"Maybe Fritz teach you lesson, hey, boy?"

"Robin! I was wondering where you wandered off to."

Robin and Fritz jerked around to see Mr. Debark next to the shed. He moved away and strode over to where the two now stood facing him. "What are my best student and Mr. Fritz Gelder talking about?" Fritz was a big man, but Mr. Debark towered over him. The light from the moon cast shadows on the teacher's hawk-like face, and Robin swore he saw Fritz shrink away with each step Mr. Debark took.

"Fritz only vish boy merry Christmas and much joy."

"Well, it's late Mr. Gelder and the boy needs to get home. Come, Robin, let's talk about your assignments on the way." Robin wordlessly nodded and walked away from Fritz with Mr. Debark. "A good evening to you, Mr. Gelder," the teacher added.

Robin glanced back and saw Fritz standing beside the shed, his mouth open, not knowing what to do.

A million thoughts raced through Robin's mind at once. It was almost too much to deal with: the unknown man, Fritz, Mr. Debark. He glanced up at Mr. Debark walking beside him, then cleared his throat. "How … how did you know …?"

Mr. Debark looked down and smiled. "I happened to leave the hall seconds after you, Robin. I saw you walking quite a distance ahead. You know I have to walk the same way as you do to get home. I saw you head over in this direction, and I have to admit, I was curious about what you were up to. By the time I got close, you were in the shadows, so I stood still for a moment or two. Then you disappeared and I heard old Fritz." Mr. Debark paused. "I know Fritz and your father don't exactly see eye to eye, so when I heard him speaking to you I thought I better wander over and see what was up. He didn't seem happy with you." Mr. Debark halted and faced Robin. "He wasn't trying to harm you, was he, son?"

Robin gathered his thoughts quickly. He didn't like to lie, but he seemed to be doing it a lot lately. "Fritz doesn't like me because of my dad. I could smell homebrew on his breath, so I think he'd been drinking. I thought I heard him talking to someone, and I snuck over to the shed. But when I came around the corner there was only old Fritz. I guess he thought I was spying on him or something. He got pretty upset and began talking about my dad and saying I was his little RCMP spy."

"Robin, he didn't intend to hurt you, did he?"

"No, sir, I don't think so. Like I said, I think he

just had too much homebrew."

They moved forward again and soon reached the edge of the compound, where they stopped before going their separate ways. "Robin, if there's anything you want to talk about ..."

"No, there's nothing really," Robin said too quickly, staring at his feet.

"Well, remember, son, I always have time for one of my best students."

Robin looked up in surprise.

Seeing the expression on Robin's face, Mr. Debark continued. "Oh, I know it might not seem like that to you, but I know you're a good student." He paused. "An excellent student, actually. You just take the easy way a little too often. You're capable of so much more, and that's why I push you so much. You get high seventies without even trying. If you applied yourself, you'd be in the nineties all the time. I'm harder on you because I want you to find your potential. I know that might not seem fair, but it's the truth. You, Wayne, and Mr. Parch are all very capable and gifted young men."

For the first time Robin saw Mr. Debark in a different light. His hard, sharp features seemed to soften, and those steely eyes appeared to glow with gentleness. Robin felt a certain amount of embarrassment about all the things he had said about the teacher. "I'll try harder, sir. I'll try to do better."

Mr. Debark put his hand on Robin's shoulder. "That's all I can ask, son. But you won't just try to do better, you will do better. I know you will." Mr. Debark turned to go, stopped, and looked back. "And just because we had this conversation, Robin, don't you dare tell Frank Firth that my Debark is worse than my debite!" He smiled and slowly ambled away, eventually disappearing into the shadows.

Robin watched long after Mr. Debark had vanished from sight. Had all of this really just happened? It was almost impossible to handle. Fritz was wrapped up in the mystery at Shildii Rock. Whoever was hiding up there knew who the boys were and what they were up to. And to top things off, Mr. Debark thought he was an excellent student. Robin pinched himself to make sure he wasn't having another dream. "Ouch!" The guys would never believe all of this!

Chapter 12

Christmas holidays were underway, and the boys had time together each day. Wayne's and Timothy's mouths dropped open when Robin told them about his encounter with Fritz and the mystery man. Their mouths gaped even farther when they heard about Mr. Debark and what he had said.

"I can't believe he's actually human!" Wayne gasped.

Robin grinned. "He called us very capable and gifted young men." The other two boys couldn't believe their ears. It was strange but true. Although the boys were enjoying the holiday season, they now had the weird sensation of looking forward to school commencing so they could see this new Mr. Debark first-hand.

The meeting with Fritz also had them itching for another trip to Shildii Rock, but the opportunity didn't present itself. Ted was busy with Dana and the dog team checking on several elders who hadn't come in from camp for the holiday season. He allowed Robin several short runs with the dogs each day to get ready for the big New Year's race, but nothing any longer. Timothy and Wayne would ride in the toboggan to provide some extra weight when Robin trained the dogs. Ted told the boys that with Dana at lead the dogs were actually training Robin. They all laughed but realized that Ted was telling the truth.

The New Year's Festival had several events: the rifle shoot, snowshoe races, and the big dog team race. All three boys were participating in the festival — Wayne in the rifle shoot, Timothy in the snowshoe competition and, of course, Robin in the dog team race.

When the big day arrived, Wayne found out that he would be among the first of the boys to compete. The rifle shoot for twelve- to sixteen-year-olds would be the initial event of the day. As things turned out, there wasn't much competition and Wayne easily took first place. Out of ten shots he had four bull's-eyes and six shots in the centre.

Timothy was in for a tougher time. The snowshoe race was three miles long, and the twelve- to sixteen-year-old category was a tough go for a thirteen-year-old. Timothy started near the back of the pack but worked his way towards the front over the first mile. With little more than a mile to go, he moved into second place behind Danny Francis.

Danny was sixteen and was big and strong. With a comfortable lead on Timothy, he kept a relaxed stride and confidently moved towards the finish. He never saw Timothy coming until it was too late. With a sprinter's finish, Timothy closed the gap and moved up beside Danny before the other boy knew what was happening. Although he was surprised, Danny managed to lunge at the finish, and both he and Timothy flew across the line and landed in a heap.

Everyone held their breath as John Kay, Robert Alexi, and Henri Bertrand huddled to decide who had won the race. Chief Kay finally stepped forward. "The judges have talked this over, and we all agree. By the tip of a snowshoe, the winner is ... Timothy Parch!"

Robin and Wayne went wild, jumped on their friend, and fell in a pile in the snow. Danny didn't stick around. Angrily, he moved off to get ready for the dog team race.

"Now we have two firsts," Timothy said, smiling. "You have to make it three, Robin."

"I won't get anything if I don't get ready," Robin said. Waving to his friends, he rushed off to get Dana and the team set.

The dogs could feel the excitement of their human handlers. Teams stood barking and tugging at their traces, nervous and anxious for the competition ahead. Some teams began to fight among themselves and had to be separated by their owners.

Dana was quiet and strong. Captain, Louie, Colonel, Corp, Sarg, and old Brig were ready behind her. As Robin approached, Dana stood and barked once. Robin knelt and scratched her behind the ears. Contentedly, she opened her mouth and gave Robin a big, wet kiss with her tongue.

"Let's do this, Dana," Robin whispered in her ear. "Let's show Danny Francis what we can do."

"Are you ready, Robin?" Ted asked as he approached his son.

"You bet I am, Dad! I know we can win this."

Ted nodded. "If you let her, Dana will win this for you. Just give her a little direction and you'll be fine."

Robin hopped onto the back of the toboggan and moved the team to the starting line. There were fourteen teams in the twelve- to sixteen-year-old class this year. Robin was the youngest musher, but everyone knew he had the best team. Danny Francis pulled his team up beside Robin and settled his dogs for the start.

The race would cover a five-mile course. They would head from the river up through town. After curling back over onto the river, they would circle an island and then head for the finish.

"Let's go, Robin!" Wayne and Timothy shouted.

Robin smiled but didn't wave. He didn't want

to look too confident and jinx himself. He ran through the course in his mind. If he could get the lead heading around the island, it would be hard for anyone to catch him.

The new constable, Grant Abernathy, had been selected as the official starter, and he moved ahead of the teams to get ready. The teams stood at the starting line as Constable Abernathy raised the red starter's flag. Mushers nervously held their teams back as they stared intently at the flag. The dogs tugged at their traces and barked excitedly. One team lunged ahead and had to be given time to return to the starting line.

Suddenly, without warning, Constable Abernathy flipped the red flag down. It seemed as if all the teams paused for a second, then the race was on. With cheers from the crowd, the dog teams dashed across the ice and up towards the centre of town. Danny Francis and his team had a quick start and immediately cut Robin's team off. Dana had to sidestep or be bumped by Danny's toboggan. With Danny cutting him off, Robin and his team were immediately hemmed in by the other teams from all sides.

As the teams moved off the river and onto the main trail through town, Robin found himself in sixth place. Panic gripped his chest, and he realized he had to settle down. With four miles left in the race, Danny was still clearly in the lead. As they wove through town, the team in front of

Robin swung too wide on a corner. Robin moved inside and jumped into fifth place. He could see Danny opening a big lead on the rest of the pack and knew he had to make up ground quickly on the next straightaway. Robin urged the team on. "Okay, Dana, go! Pull, Brig! Captain, Louie, go now!"

Robin's team pulled hard. By the time the racers passed through town, he was creeping into third place. Robin knew the trail well and realized they would soon be back on the river headed for the island turnaround. A final hill lay just before the descent back onto the river. If Robin remembered correctly, the trail veered severely to the left over the hill. The team in front of Robin was taking the trail just about in the middle. If Robin was right and took the left side, he would come out ahead over the hill. If he was wrong, he could end up off the trail or run into spectators and trees.

In a split second Robin made his decision and shifted left. As the toboggan lifted over the hill, Robin saw a tree immediately ahead. He had guessed correctly but was too far left! Before he could utter a word, Dana smoothly took the team to the inside of the tree, then carried left around the turn. Robin's shoulder slammed against the tree, spinning him off the back of the toboggan. Gripping hard with his right hand, he pulled himself upright and back into position.

His gamble had paid off! He was now in second place. His shoulder pounded with pain, but he concentrated on the musher directly in front of him — Danny Francis!

The two lead teams curled back through town and hurtled towards the river, passing the starting line, which would also serve as the finish. A huge crowd had gathered there. The spectators' cheers and shouts, though, seemed far away as Robin concentrated on finishing the race. He was now only two toboggan lengths behind Danny.

As Robin swept past Wayne and Timothy, his friends went wild. Everyone watched as the teams rushed across the ice and disappeared behind the island. Seconds seemed like minutes as the crowd waited anxiously for the two teams to come back into sight on the other side. With an eighth of a mile remaining, whoever had the lead at this stage would have a considerable advantage.

Wayne jumped in the air and hugged Timothy as first Dana and then Louie and the whole team came into view. But Danny wasn't far behind. Ted Harris moved to the front of the crowd. Placing two fingers in his mouth, he whistled loud and clear. The whistle from her master made Dana bolt. The team moved faster, and the crowd saw Robin's lead grow by the second. The race was his!

Robin was filled with excitement and couldn't

contain a giddy laugh. He had done it! Dana had done it! He didn't see the drift until it was too late. Hardened by wind on the open river, it acted like a jump. The toboggan hit at full force and tipped. Robin splayed onto the ice but managed to hang on to the toboggan with his left hand. Frantically, he tried to stretch his right hand to the lazy-back, but it was no use. Slowly, his grip loosened and he let go. He felt the head rope pull under his body and made one desperate attempt to snatch it. His mitt closed on the rope, but then it was gone.

Looking up from the ice and snow, Robin spied Dana and the team racing towards the finish line with the toboggan dragging on its side. Danny Francis and his team were only a blur to Robin as he watched them pass, his eyes full of tears. He sat in the snow and sobbed as several other teams sped past. A team had to finish with its rider or it was disqualified. Not only had Robin lost the race, he hadn't even finished!

Removing his mitt and wiping his eyes, he got to his feet and shuffled towards the finish. Wayne and Timothy ran out to meet him. Timothy looked devastated, and Wayne was openly crying. "That was your race," he cried.

"I know," Robin mumbled. "I never saw it coming. I thought I'd won the race and I guess I kind of let up. I have no one to blame but myself."

Timothy and Wayne each put an arm around

Robin and accompanied him to the finish line. A crowd had gathered around Danny Francis, but he moved to meet the boys as they approached. Stopping in front of Robin, he held out his hand. "You deserved to win that race, Robin. You were the better driver and you had the better team."

"Thanks," Robin said, lost for any other words as he shook Danny's hand.

The older boy grinned. "You'll win easy next year."

Robin nodded as Danny walked away. Danny's words did make him feel a bit better. Robin searched the crowd for his father, surprised he hadn't greeted him at the finish. Then he spotted his father talking to Constable Abernathy, Johnny Reindeer, and Ben Vittrekwa. As Robin approached, they stopped speaking. Ted stared at Robin, his mouth tight.

Robin avoided eye contact. "I'm sorry, Dad. I know I let you down. I … well —"

"I'm not mad at you, Robin. You mushed a heck of a race. There's something else far more serious than this dog race. Ben just came in from camp. He found Fritz on the trail this morning near Rock River. Son, Fritz is dead."

Chapter 13

Word of the Dutchman's death travelled fast in Fort McPherson and was the subject of every conversation in every home. Apparently, Ben Vittrekwa had come across Fritz's body on a trail south of Rock River. It appeared to Ben that a tree had fallen onto the trail and struck the trapper in the head. Although it was too late to help Fritz, Ben had brought him back to town. Ben had felt something wasn't right in the bush where he had found the Dutchman. When Ted examined Fritz, he got the same impression. They would have to make the trip to the location where Ben had discovered Fritz to complete the investigation.

Using the RCMP single-side band radio, Ted radioed Aklavik and spoke to Inspector Limpkert, his supervisor. The inspector thought Ted was overreacting, but he agreed to fly in to lead the investigation.

Robin, Wayne, and Timothy wondered if Fritz's death had anything to do with the strange conversation Robin had heard the night of the Christmas feast. They struggled once again with the decision to tell Ted what they had turned up at Shildii Rock. In the end they chose to stay quiet. Ted had told the boys that Fritz's death seemed to be an accident. If they told Ted their story now and it was indeed an accident, they would look pretty silly.

Late the next morning after daylight, Jack Wainwright flew Inspector Limpkert from Aklavik to Fort McPherson. There was no airstrip, so the plane landed on the Peel River. Ted picked up the inspector with the dog team and returned to the office.

The boys were determined to hear what the inspector had to say. Much to his disappointment, Timothy had to assist his father at the store once more, but Robin and Wayne did their best to learn everything they could. They were at the office with Johnny and Constable Abernathy when Ted and Inspector Limpkert arrived. Sitting in the background and trying to remain unnoticed, they listened as the men discussed their next course of action.

Inspector Limpkert was a thin, humourless man who liked to demonstrate his authority. He wore his jet-black hair cropped short and greased back. His pencil-thin moustache could have been painted beneath his nose. Robin always imagined him spending hours in front of a mirror trimming it to get it right. Now the inspector stood before the other men, hands firmly planted on his hips. He didn't seem to acknowledge Johnny or the boys' presence and directed all of his questions at Ted and Constable Abernathy, who were sitting at their desks.

"And this Ben Vittrekwa, Corporal, is he a reliable Native?"

Ted shifted uneasily in his chair. "Ben's a reliable *man,* sir. He knows the bush and he has good sense. If he feels something wasn't quite right, we should investigate."

"Hmmph!" Inspector Limpkert snorted as he began to pace.

Robin pictured the inspector as a weasel sitting upright, ready to run for cover at the slightest sign of trouble. He stifled a snicker and took a silent elbow to the ribs from Wayne.

"And what do you suggest we do, Corporal?" Inspector Limpkert asked.

"Well, sir, I believe we should head up to Rock River in the morning. Rock River's about thirty-five miles southwest, and Fritz's camp about another twenty. We can overnight on the way there and on the way back. Three days should do it."

"Hmmph! Well, Corporal, I disagree. We'll leave today. If we travel hard, we can make it a two-day trip."

Ted cleared his throat. "But, sir, we don't have

enough daylight. I think —"

"Reindeer!" Spinning, Inspector Limpkert faced Johnny across his desk. "Can you follow the trail in the dark?"

Johnny looked at Ted, then glanced down. "Well, yes, sir, but —"

"Fine! Then get ready, men. It's this type of sitting around with no action that'll cost us time and less daylight to travel in."

Ted knew it was no use arguing with the inspector. "Very well, sir, we'll take three teams. Ben will lead us to the spot, Johnny will take his team, and I'll bring the other. Grant will stay behind to deal with the gossip and keep things calm here in town. If it's okay with you, Inspector, Robin and Wayne will travel with us."

Both boys looked up, surprised at the mention of their names.

"Corporal, this is serious business. It's police business and no place for boys or those who can't assist with the investigation."

"Begging your pardon, sir. They're young men and very capable on the trail. If we need to break trail or have some heavy work ahead of us, they can help with the dogs. And *only* help with the dogs." Ted cast Robin and Wayne a serious look. "As far as the investigation, they'll be out of the way and not even noticed."

"Hmmph!" Inspector Limpkert glanced at the boys and marched to the office door. "It's highly irregular, Corporal. However, so is this whole wild-goose chase. Make sure they do keep out of the way. Very well, men, let's get to it!"

Chapter 14

By the time everything was ready for the trip, it was early afternoon. The days were longer, but they would still have very little real light. Ben Vittrekwa led the procession with Inspector Limpkert in his toboggan. Johnny followed with Wayne, while Ted with Robin brought up the rear.

The trail was in excellent condition and the teams made good time. They followed the Peel River due south, then cut west on Vitrequois Creek. The trail once again moved south past Stoney Creek and White Fox Creek. At this point the trail crossed into Yukon Territory and continued past Caribou House River, Sister Creek, and Timber Creek. It was dark now, but the moon was full. Ben and Johnny knew the trail well, so staying on course was no problem. It was well after 7:00 p.m. when they passed Rock River. They stopped at this point, and Ted suggested they set up camp.

"Nonsense!" Inspector Limpkert said. "We have a full moon and a clear sky. We'll continue. Now what in blazes are those two up to?"

Ben and Johnny had moved off the trail and were digging in an area where the ground was exposed. Johnny had a knapsack out and was placing something inside.

"There's a certain red ochre in the soil here, sir," Ted said. "The local people collect it to dye birch wood snowshoes and caribou hides. They believe the location is special."

"Hmmph! Let's get going, men!"

Johnny returned to his toboggan and placed the knapsack inside. Then he took a small pouch of tobacco and walked back to where he had been digging. Ben was close behind him.

"Get back here, men!" the inspector ordered. "We need to get moving!"

Johnny stopped and glanced at Ted, who cleared his throat. "Sir, the people believe that if you take the ochre, you have to leave an offering in return. If you don't, the spirits might cause bad weather or some other terrible thing."

The inspector waved Johnny and Ben back to their teams. "Nonsense! A bunch of Native mumbo-jumbo! Let's move on immediately!"

Johnny silently shook his head.

The group got underway and travelled over hard-packed snow that shone in the moonlight like a vast white ocean. The sound of the toboggans sliding over the snow soothed Robin, and his head bobbed with the onset of sleep. The weather so far had been clear and mild, but after several miles a slight wind began to blow in from the north. The temperature had been a reasonable minus eighteen, but as the wind picked up force it seemed much colder. By the time they covered another half mile, it was almost impossible to see as the wind scattered loose snow over the trail.

Admitting defeat, Inspector Limpkert gave the men permission to halt and put up their tents for the night. The wind made the task difficult, but eventually they erected two tents and secured them. The inspector and Ted bunked in one tent, while Robin and Wayne decided they would sleep in the other with Johnny and Ben. Nestled in their sleeping bags with the wind howling against the canvas, everyone was soon asleep.

At one point Robin opened his eyes, unsure if something had disturbed his sleep or if it had just been the wind shrieking. As his sight adjusted to the darkness, he spotted someone hunched just inside the door flap. Propping himself on one elbow, Robin squinted and realized it was Johnny. "Hey, Johnny!"

"*Shhhh.*" Johnny held a finger to his lips. Smiling, he raised his other hand. In it was the pouch of tobacco. "I'll be back soon." Turning, he quickly slipped out into the storm and was gone.

Robin drifted in and out of sleep. He dreamed

of wind spirits and huge birds. He floated in the clouds and rode the currents of air. When he woke sometime later, the high wind had calmed to a light breeze, gently rippling the sides of the tent. He heard a low rustling and raised his head.

Johnny entered the tent and smiled. "I thought I better take care of my mumbo-jumbo." Then, with a wink, he crept into his sleeping bag.

Robin lay back, curled up in the warmth, and began to dream again. This time he was visited by friendly spirits who rocked him gently to sleep.

Chapter 15

In the morning the weather was completely clear. Inspector Limpkert made a big speech about how the weather was now fine even though they hadn't left an offering at Rock River. Frustrated, Robin almost spoke out, but one glance at Johnny changed his mind. Even in the gloom he could see Wayne's father put a finger to his lips, smile, and shake his head.

Wayne noticed his friend fidgeting and inched up beside him. "My dad went back last night, didn't he?"

Robin nodded.

"I knew he would," Wayne whispered. "He's never wrong about these things."

The teams started off in darkness once again and didn't get any daylight until after 10:00 a.m. The going was a bit rough since the wind had drifted snow over many sections of the trail. The men took turns leading the teams on snowshoe, with the exception of Inspector Limpkert, who huddled in Ben's toboggan. Early in the afternoon Ben pulled up his team and indicated that they had reached the spot where he had found Fritz. Here the trail was relatively bare, with thick bush and trees on either side.

Inspector Limpkert, Ted, Johnny, and Ben spread out to search the area. The boys volunteered to help but were ordered by Ted to stay at the toboggans and look after the dogs. Piece by piece the men patched together a picture of what had really happened to Fritz. Despite the inspector's initial insistence that Fritz's death had been accidental, he soon had to concede that the Dutchman had indeed met with foul play. The tree that Ben thought had struck Fritz on the head had actually been cut down.

Deeper in the bushes, Johnny located a stick that had blood and some traces of hair imbedded in the bark. Carefully, Ted wrapped the stick in a cloth, knowing that it might well have delivered the fatal blow. It was Ben, however, who made the most interesting discovery. He stumbled across the stump where the tree had been cut down. Just to the left of the tree two cigarette butts lay in the snow.

Ted examined the butts closely and handed them to the inspector. "Sir, I think these are important evidence."

"Hmmph!" the inspector grunted. "Cigarette butts. Not much we can tell from them other than that the deceased might have been a smoker."

"Actually, sir," Ted said, "Fritz was many things, but to my knowledge a smoker wasn't one of them." The inspector began to speak, but Ted held up his hand. "If I could be so bold, sir, these are store-bought cigarettes. You don't see many of these up here. What's really important, though, is the cigarette brand."

As the inspector peered at the butts again, surprise and interest crossed his face. "Well, I'll be! Camel. They're American. You certainly don't find these in our neck of the woods."

Wayne and Robin exchanged worried glances. "Dad, I need to —"

"Not now, son," Ted said. "We need to head back to town and start asking some questions." He turned to the inspector. "I'm not aware, sir, of anyone from the States being in this area. Perhaps the stores or —"

"I know someone!"

Everyone stared at Robin where he stood beside Wayne.

Robin studied his feet, then glanced at Wayne. "Actually, *we* know someone, Dad."

Ted gave his son a stern look. "Robin, this isn't the time for one of your stories. If you really know something, you better tell us now."

"Let the boy speak, Corporal," the inspector said. Moving over to Robin and Wayne, he considered the boys intently. "Just what do you two know?"

Taking a deep breath, Robin told the inspector what they had found and seen. Throughout Robin's story Wayne nodded whenever his name was mentioned and tried to avoid eye contact with his father who he knew would be furious at their deceit. The Montana matches, the camp, the cave, the man with the strange accent, the Christmas feast encounter with Fritz — Robin didn't spare any details. When he finished, he looked up, trying to judge how much trouble he was in by the expression on his father's face. However, it was Inspector Limpkert who spoke first.

"My God, son, this is incredible. You knew all of this and you didn't tell your father? This is next to obstruction of justice!"

"Sir, don't blame the boy." All eyes turned to Ted. "He tried to tell me at first, but I didn't listen. If anyone obstructed justice, it was me. I guess we've both learned something, son. I have to trust your intuitions more, and you have to come up with a few less stories so we believe more of the real things you see." Ted managed a weak smile and shook his head.

"It's my fault, too," Johnny added. "When I took the boys out to Shildii Rock, I had a pretty good idea they were up to something. But I treated them like silly boys. They're men now and we have to respect them as men."

Both fathers regarded their sons with silent pride.

"Well, now that you've all accepted blame, how in blazes do we get to this Shildii Rock!" Inspector Limpkert stood with his hands on his hips. "Based on what these boys have told us, my guess is someone's trying to lead us away from this Shildii Rock. Fritz knew too much, so he became part of this Yank's plan to keep something secret."

Ted moved closer to the inspector. "Shildii is back down the Peel River, sir. We passed it not far from Fort McPherson. We're already losing daylight. May I suggest we start back to town and camp within a few hours of Shildii? If we plan our start in the morning, we can get to Shildii while our light's at its best."

The inspector nodded. "Now you're thinking, Corporal. Let's get cracking. We've got a mystery to solve."

Chapter 16

Robin thought it was the longest trip he had ever taken in his life. It seemed to take days to travel back to Shildii Rock. That night, after they made camp, the men discussed how to approach Shildii and what to do if they met with resistance. They had no way of contacting Constable Abernathy, so Inspector Limpkert and Ted would have to control the situation if they encountered the individual they were looking for.

Ted and the inspector made sure their service revolvers were in good working order. Watching the men prepare for the worst filled Robin and Wayne with a combination of excitement and fear. They sensed the tension shared by the four adults, which made for a long, uneasy night of broken sleep.

In the morning they set out for Shildii Rock. Their timing was perfect, and daylight was gaining strength as they pulled up on the shore below their destination. Once again the boys remained with the dogs while the men went above to investigate the camp. Wayne and Robin wanted to go along but realized how dangerous the situation was. Still, no matter what the circumstances were, the boys longed to be part of the action.

The men climbed the bank and wove their way through the bush. The boys had provided good directions and the trail was easy to find. Both Ted and the inspector unbuckled the holster covers on their Sam Browne belts so they could easily access their revolvers if necessary. Johnny and Ben, their rifles ready for whatever might happen, followed. At the sight of the camp all four men huddled to finalize their approach.

"We don't want to scare anyone into taking rash action," Inspector Limpkert informed the group. "I'll identify who we are to the camp and we'll wait to see if we can't reason with this character. After all, this might just be a coincidence."

Clearing his throat, the inspector stood and moved to the edge of the bush across from the camp. "To anyone who can hear me! This is Inspector Limpkert of the Royal Canadian Mounted Police. I'm here with Corporal Ted Harris and some others. We'd like to talk to you. We mean you no harm. We just want to speak to you!"

The silence that followed was chilling. Looking back at the men, the inspector shrugged. Then he turned back to the camp and shouted, "Hello in there! This is —"

With a loud crack the tree branch directly above the inspector's head exploded. He fell to the ground and rolled onto his back. "I'm guessing that meant the Yank doesn't want to talk to us!"

Ted smiled despite himself and crouched lower beside Johnny and Ben. Two more gunshots sprayed snow on either side of the inspector. Then Ben pointed and cried, "Over there!"

The men spotted a rifle barrel just visible at the edge of the rock embankment where the boys had indicated the cave was located. Ted held his revolver steady and fired twice. He shot high above the location of the rifle. "Those were warning shots! Stop now and come out with your hands up before we —"

Three rapid shots sent Ted diving for cover. Both Johnny and Ben levelled their rifles and fired. Branches in the bush snapped as their bullets ripped through the undergrowth. Then all was silent.

The inspector joined the other men and sprawled beside them, low to the ground. "Cover me, boys. I'm going to try to outflank him. Ted, Johnny, Ben, are you ready?"

"Yes, sir!" they all chimed.

"On three. One, two ... *three!*" The inspector ran in a crouch as Ted, Johnny, and Ben fired from their positions. Diving for cover, the inspector waved to his men, then was on his feet again, dodging out of sight around the corner of the rock towards the cave.

The first gunshot jolted Robin and Wayne to attention. They looked at each other, too afraid to speak.

"What should we do?" Robin finally squeaked.

"I don't know," Wayne said, his voice quavering. "Stay here I guess. Do you think we should go up top?"

Robin gulped. *"No!"*

They heard more gunshots, but all they could do was stand, wait, and try to guess what was going on at the camp. Then there were more shots and finally silence.

Chapter 17

To Wayne and Robin it seemed as if years had passed between the last gunshot and the noise they now heard. Someone was crashing through the bushes upriver! The boys stood frozen, not knowing who it was or what to do.

"Boys, look out! Robin, run! Run, boys!" Ted yelled from above.

They were both terrified. Running was the easiest thing to do, but they didn't. Instead they both had the same thought at exactly the same time. Dana!

Running to the toboggan, Wayne and Robin worked furiously together and had Dana out of her harness in seconds.

"Get him, Dana!" Robin screamed. "Sic him now!"

Dana had sensed that things were wrong. She smelled the human fear in the air and recognized the boys' panic. At a full run before Robin finished speaking, she closed the gap between herself and the bush within seconds and leaped with all her strength as the figure crashed into sight from the willows. He never had a chance. With a scream he fell to the ground, his rifle clattering across the snow. Dana bit hard and began to shake her victim as hard as possible.

"Get it off! Help! Stop it from eating me! *Ahhhhhh!*"

Johnny and Ted broke through the willows and stopped abruptly on the shore. Ben and the inspector were right behind them. They all gasped for breath, staring at the scene that lay before them. A man sat on the shore sobbing, his hands covering his face. Wayne stood slightly back, guarding him with his own rifle, while Robin held Dana back by the collar about a foot from where the fugitive slumped.

"Well, I'll be jiggered!" Inspector Limpkert exclaimed. "You were right about these boys, Corporal. They sure can handle themselves."

"I guess I was, sir," Ted said with a dazed smile. "More than I ever imagined."

Ted strode over to the prisoner and stood him off the snow. Forcing the man's hands behind his back, he slipped on handcuffs and let the prisoner sag back onto the snow. Dana barked and lunged at the man where he sat. He shouted with fear and skittered crablike across the snow away from the dog.

Inspector Limpkert stepped forward and

grabbed the man by the arm. "Would you mind telling us your name, what you're doing here, and why you shot at us?"

The man glared at the snow and shook his head. "I should have taken care of those kids and that dog myself," he muttered.

"I don't think we'll get much out of him right now, sir," Ted said. "Perhaps we should inspect and secure the campsite before heading back to town."

"Excellent, Corporal. Let's get to it!"

With Johnny, Ben, and the boys watching the prisoner, Ted and Inspector Limpkert worked their way back up to the camp. It took some time as they followed the route the man had taken through the bush just in case he had discarded evidence as he ran. When they returned a while later, they had gathered everything they would need.

"I think we'll have a pretty straightforward case," the inspector said, turning to the group and their prisoner. "We found several items that can be identified as belonging to one Fritz Gelder — a pocketknife with his initials engraved in the handle, a pocket watch with Mr. Gelder's name on it, and some tools with his initials. We also have several packs of cigarettes. Camels to be exact! I'm guessing these are the only Camel cigarettes we'll find for at least a thousand miles in any direction." The inspector stopped and glanced at Ted. "And we have one other item that's the most interesting of all, right, Corporal?"

Ted moved closer to the group and took a small pouch the size of a marble bag out of a pocket in his parka. Loosening the drawstrings, he carefully shook some of the contents into the palm of his hand. Everyone crowded around to get a better look at the small objects shining in Ted's open hand.

Robin had never seen anything like them before, but he knew exactly what they were. "Diamonds!" he gasped. "Those are diamonds, aren't they?"

"Yes, indeed, son," Ted said. "They're diamonds. And they're the real mystery Shildii Rock's been guarding all these years. You can touch one if you like, but be careful. If we drop any, we'll never find them in the snow."

The boys didn't need any coaxing. They both gently took one of the gems and held them up for inspection. In the sunset light of an arctic winter day, the diamonds glistened with all the colours of a rainbow.

"So this is what it was all about," Robin said in a hushed voice.

Chapter 18

Fort McPherson was in an uproar. The next morning Inspector Limpkert held a public meeting at the community hall to answer questions and give real answers to all the rumours circulating around town. The little building was packed, with standing room only. Robin, Wayne, and Timothy arrived late and remained at the back near Timothy's father, watching the inspector where he stood at the front with Ted, Johnny, Constable Abernathy, and Ben.

After quieting the crowd, the inspector explained what had happened to Fritz and assured everybody that the perpetrator was in custody. He also explained some things the boys hadn't realized.

"The man we have in custody is Donald McCathery. There's no doubt he's responsible for what happened to Fritz Gelder. We've learned from headquarters that McCathery is wanted in the United States for several crimes, including murder and armed robbery. In fact, he's on the FBI's Most Wanted List. There's a reward for his capture, but we'll get to that later.

"The cave McCathery found was no doubt once inhabited by the Gwich'in — possibly centuries ago. The entrance was overgrown, and it wasn't until McCathery came along that its true treasure was discovered. How McCathery found it, we're not exactly sure, and he isn't about to tell us. It's quite possible that Fritz found the cave first and told McCathery about it later. We found several Gwich'in artifacts in the cave that will be returned to the community once the investigation is complete.

"There are small amounts of diamonds in the cave. They're right on the surface of the cave floor and easy to locate. In all probability diamonds will be found below the surface as well if the cave is mined. For now these diamonds are the property of the Canadian government until the matter of mineral rights and other details have been investigated."

Inspector Limpkert surveyed the crowd. Spying the boys at the back, he smiled thinly, then once more became serious. "Now, as to the matter of the criminal's capture, I'd first like to recognize the excellent work of Corporal Ted Harris, Special Constable Johnny Reindeer, and Ben Vittrekwa. They were all faced with grave danger and were heroic beyond the call of duty for police officers or civilians. Men, I salute you." With that announcement Inspector Limpkert snapped to attention and saluted the men standing beside him. "There are also other brave individuals who deserve the highest of recognition in relation to this case. First, I'd like to call upon police dog Dana Anxious Sheba to come forward."

Everyone turned as Marjorie Harris led Dana in from the back of the hall. When Robin's mother released the dog's collar, Dana padded to the front and calmly sat beside Ted, who patted her affectionately on the head and scratched behind her ears.

The inspector harrumphed, then continued. "Dana was responsible for the final apprehension of the criminal and will be recognized for her bravery and dedication to the police force." Once again the inspector snapped to attention. Then he turned to Dana and saluted her. Sitting upright, Dana barked loudly, causing ripples of laughter and applause throughout the crowd.

The inspector stifled his own laughter, then said, "Now to the matter of three other heroes. I'd like to call Wayne Reindeer, Timothy Parch, and Robin Harris to the front, please."

The three boys glanced at one another in surprise. Self-consciously, they made their way through the crowd and halted in front of the inspector. Wayne looked at his father, who smiled back. Robin gazed at Ted, who winked.

"Without these three young men," the inspector said, "solving this case wouldn't have been possible. Through their solid detective work they were actually on the fugitive's trail well before we were aware of the situation. Wayne, Timothy, and Robin uncovered strange circumstances at Shildii Rock and gathered information that was key to our investigation. In the end, Wayne and Robin led us to the cave and, along with Dana, apprehended the fugitive. I would now like to salute these three young gentlemen and present them with letters of commendation signed by myself on behalf of the Royal Canadian Mounted Police."

Inspector Limpkert snapped to attention and saluted Wayne before presenting him with his letter. He repeated this procedure with Timothy and finally Robin. The crowd burst into cheers and applause as the three boys stood sheepishly at the front, their faces a mix of excitement and embarrassment. When Robin spotted Mr. Debark near the back of the room, he was thrilled when the teacher nodded his approval. The inspector joined in the applause and then held up his hand for silence. The crowd settled down and he continued.

"Now there's one other matter that remains to be settled. And that's the reward." He paused and watched as the boys once again exchanged surprised looks. "Yes, the reward. The FBI has posted a reward of $1,000 for anyone who assists in the apprehension of Mr. McCathery. Seeing as it's against the policy of the RCMP for any of its officers to accept rewards or honours for carrying out their duties, the reward will be split four ways. Ben Vittrekwa, Wayne Reindeer, Timothy Parch, and Robin Harris will each receive $250 for their part in the capture of the fugitive."

At those words the room erupted with cheers. The three boys laughed and grabbed one another by the arms.

"This is unbelievable!" Timothy shouted above the noise.

"Man, just think of what we can buy with that much cash!" Wayne yelled.

"Ouch!" Robin blurted.

Timothy and Wayne stopped chuckling and stared at their friend.

"Sorry, guys, it's just that I've dreamt about this stuff so much I had to pinch myself to make sure I'm awake."

Wayne and Timothy grabbed Robin and mussed up his hair.

When the boys made their way out of the hall, everyone shook their hands and congratulated them. It felt good, and they took their time leaving. Once outside, they walked abreast through town — three friends with grins on their faces and thoughts of reward money dancing in their brains.

"This has got to be the best thing that's ever happened to me," Timothy said.

"It's pretty special, isn't it?" Wayne agreed.

They both looked at Robin, who remained silent. He was staring off towards the mountains and appeared deep in thought. "You know, guys, now that we've got some time to ourselves, I've been meaning to tell you something. When I was picking cloudberries last fall with my mother, I saw these strange tracks just downriver. If I can get Dana and the team from Dad maybe —"

"No way!" Timothy groaned.

"Get him!" Wayne shouted.

Robin ran as fast as he could, with his two friends in hot pursuit.

Ted Harris stood with Johnny on the steps of the community hall. Sighing, he asked Johnny, "Do you think they'll ever change?"

"I sure hope not!"

The two men smiled at each other and watched the boys chase one another in the fading light of a perfect northern winter afternoon.